"Maybe this was Reid said.

"What?"

"Coming back to Stampede."

Scarlett's heart sank. The last thing she'd meant to do was discourage Reid from staying in town, especially when he hadn't been home in over a decade. "You can't leave." She winced at the eager note in her voice. "Being with family will play in your favor when the social worker decides whether or not you should be given permanent custody of Jessie."

"Got any other reasons why I shouldn't leave?"

She shook her head. "That's it, why?"

His mouth curved into a smile. "I thought maybe you'd want to judge for yourself if my kissing has improved."

"Well, there is that, too." Scarlett smiled.

His blue eyes darkened. "I really like you, Scarlett."

Reid's declaration wasn't all that swoon-worthy but for a woman who dealt with the ugly side of life on a daily basis, it was a beacon of sunshine filled with hope and possibilities.

Dear Reader,

I'm so excited to share Reid Hardell's story with you! If you've read the previous two books in my Cowboys of Stampede, Texas series (*The Cowboy's Accidental Baby* and *Twins for the Texas Rancher*) then you know that Reid is the black sheep of the Hardell family and he made a conscious choice years ago to keep his distance.

I've always been fascinated by family secrets—we all have them. In *Lone Star Father* Reid Hardell is heading home to Paradise Ranch because he's looking for help raising a daughter he never knew existed until recently. He knows the homecoming won't be the stuff of fairy tales, but the last thing he expects to find waiting for him at the ranch is another family secret and a woman who quickly becomes more than just his daughter's social worker.

It's Scarlett Johnson's intention to help Reid and Jessie bond, but her heart keeps getting in the way of her job. As Reid and Scarlett consider what's best for everyone concerned, they discover the only real way forward is together—as a family.

I invite you to check out all of my books at marinthomas.com where you can also sign up for my newsletter and find links to connect with me on social media.

Happy reading,

Marin

LONE STAR FATHER

Marin Thomas

HARLEQUIN® WESTERN ROMANCE

Recycling programs
for this product may
not exist in your area.

ISBN-13: 978-1-335-69972-5

Lone Star Father

Printed in U.S.A.

www.Harlequin.com

Marin Thomas grew up in the Midwest, then attended college at the U of A in Tucson, Arizona, where she earned a BA in radio-TV and played basketball for the Lady Wildcats. Following graduation, she married her college sweetheart in the historic Little Chapel of the West in Las Vegas, Nevada. Recent empty-nesters, Marin and her husband now live in Texas, where cattle is king, cowboys are plentiful and pickups rule the road. Visit her on the web at marinthomas.com.

Books by Marin Thomas

Harlequin Western Romance

The Cowboys of Stampede, Texas

The Cowboy's Accidental Baby
Twins for the Texas Rancher

Harlequin American Romance

Cowboys of the Rio Grande

A Cowboy's Redemption
The Surgeon's Christmas Baby
A Cowboy's Claim

The Cash Brothers

The Cowboy Next Door
Twins Under the Christmas Tree
Her Secret Cowboy
The Cowboy's Destiny
True Blue Cowboy
A Cowboy of Her Own

Visit the Author Profile page
at Harlequin.com for more titles.

For Cristina and Tom—dedicated social workers who spend their days and sometimes nights helping at-risk children and teenagers.

And for Marin—a clinical psychologist who spends countless hours helping veterans and individuals suffering from PTSD and trauma-related disorders.

The world would be better off with more people like you.

Chapter One

Becoming a father was not something Reid Hardell had ever imagined for himself, especially twelve years after the fact.

The social worker's voice echoed in his ear. *Mr. Hardell, I realize this situation caught you by surprise, but you're the only family Jessie has left.*

Family.

His stomach churned as the word reverberated inside his head.

At half past midnight, he flipped on the blinker and took the exit for Stampede. He could only imagine the looks on the faces of his grandfather and brothers when Reid introduced them to his daughter. He should have warned the family that he was returning home to Texas and why, but he'd barely kept in touch with them since entering the military after high school.

Reid had always felt like an outsider in his family and had never figured out why his father had come down harder on him than his two brothers. His jaw tightened at the memory of the old man shoving him to the ground, then kicking dirt in his face, after Reid had asked for the keys to his truck so he could take a girl to the movies. Later that night his older brother, Logan, had driven off in the pickup with his friends.

When Reid's enlistment in the marines was up, he hadn't returned to Paradise Ranch. Instead, he'd chosen to settle in Albuquerque. It hadn't made sense to go back to a place which held few good memories.

He glanced across the seat at his daughter—the reason Reid was making this trip. Six months had passed since he'd met Jessie in September, but her name still rolled off his tongue like a boulder. He was floundering in his role as her dad and he was looking to his siblings to help him navigate fatherhood.

Any day now Reid's younger brother, Gunner, was going to become a first-time father and Logan had recently married a single mother with twin boys. Surely they could give him a few pointers on parenting.

Reid's gaze shifted to the urn propped on the seat next to Jessie. Her mother was making the eight-hour drive with them from El Paso to Stampede, an hour south of San Antonio. He'd suggested spreading the ashes before they'd left Jessie's foster home, but she hadn't been ready to say goodbye to her mother. He understood. Sort of.

His father's sudden death had cheated him out having the last word. A few weeks after Reid left for boot camp, a hit-and-run driver had killed Donny Hardell while he changed a flat tire on the side of the road. Reid remembered the phone call from his grandfather as if it had happened yesterday. First, Reid had been numb with shock, then he'd felt weightless—as if the heavy sensation resting on his chest most of his life had broken apart and vanished. His grandfather hadn't revealed the funeral arrangements and Reid hadn't asked. They both knew he wouldn't be paying his respects to a man who'd treated him with contempt.

His gaze flicked to the rearview mirror, where the corner of the glass displayed the outside temperature—fifty-nine degrees. Typical mid-March weather in the Lone Star State. He set the cruise control and lifted his aching foot from the gas pedal. He should have removed his cowboy boots and put on his athletic shoes earlier in the day, but each time they'd stopped for a break, Reid had been distracted. Twice the dog had bolted from the truck when Jessie opened the door and they'd had to capture him. Then Jessie had asked for a snack from a vending machine that ate her money. And the bathrooms at two of the rest stops had been out of order, requiring a detour.

Soft snoring sounds drifted into his ear and he glanced into the back seat. Fang slept soundly in the dog bed on top of the luggage. The five-year-old short-haired golden Chihuahua with half its teeth missing had belonged to the Valentines—the elderly foster parents who'd taken Jessie in after Stacy died. According to the couple, Fang and Jessie had a special bond, which Reid had witnessed when the mutt escaped the yard and chased his pickup down the street after they'd driven off earlier in the day. When they'd returned the dog to its owners, Jessie had begun crying and then so did Mrs. Valentine. Finally, Mr. Valentine shoved the mutt into Reid's arms and said, "He's Jessie's now."

The three of them were an unlikely family, but... Reid lost his thought when the word *family* reverberated inside his head again. The Hardells had been no more or no less dysfunctional than most families but Reid had decided in the military that he'd never marry or have kids. He didn't want to be a dad. After the way his father had treated him, he had no idea how to nurture a kid's mental or emotional well-being.

So much for the promise you made yourself.

Reid gripped the wheel tighter as he drove past his family's rural property. He had tried to earn his father's approval by showing an interest in his dad's hobby—working on car engines. All he'd gotten for his efforts had been a dressing-down. Reid had developed a real aptitude for mechanics and by the age of seventeen he'd fixed engines his father hadn't been able to get running—still his old man had always found fault with Reid's work.

After he left the military, he'd landed a job as a mechanic for a trucking company in Duke City and had made a life for himself away from his family. A life that had been turned around when a social worker in El Paso informed him that he might be the biological father of a twelve-year-old girl.

A beacon of light appeared up ahead—the Moonlight Motel. A full moon spun in a slow circle atop a forty-foot pole and the word Vacancy glowed blue against the white backdrop. Last summer Gunner had texted Reid the link to the Moonlight's website and Reid had viewed before-and-after pictures of the newly renovated motel.

He turned into the lot, surprised to see vehicles in front of the rooms. Years ago, the motel had sat empty most days. He parked by the office and shut off the engine. He didn't notice anyone behind the check-in desk. Maybe Gunner was in the back playing video games or watching TV. He reached for his cowboy hat only to discover Fang had flipped it over and crawled inside the crown to sleep.

Great. His head would smell like dog the next time

he wore the hat. He left the pickup, closing the door quietly. After *hello*, he had no idea what he'd say to his brother. His heart pounding like a jackhammer, he stared at his boots as he walked across the pavement.

The surge of adrenaline racing through his bloodstream caused him to pull the handle harder than he intended. The door flew open and a body slammed into his chest. His quick reflexes kicked in and he wrapped his arms around his assailant. When a pair of soft breasts pressed against him, he stumbled backward, his shoulder hitting the doorjamb.

"Oh, my, gosh." The woman extricated herself from his hold and backed up. She brushed a lock of blond hair from her brown eyes. "I'm so sorry." She flashed a smile. He'd seen a photo of Gunner's wife and Lydia had long hair. This woman had really short hair. He opened his mouth to introduce himself, but Fang started yipping and barking and a moment later his daughter got out of the vehicle.

Jessie rubbed her eyes. "What's going on?"

"We're in Stampede." Reid looked at the blonde. "My daughter and I need a room for the night if there's one available."

When Jessie fetched Fang from the back seat and attached his leash, the woman pointed to a pathway between the motel rooms and the office. "Follow the sidewalk. There's a patch of grass back there."

Left alone with the petite woman whose sultry eyes were way too big for her face, Reid apologized. "I'm sorry. You weren't hurt, were you?"

"I'm fine."

He preferred long hair on women but the shorter style with wispy bangs drew his attention to her pretty

eyes and high cheekbones. When his gaze dropped to
her mouth, her lips spread into a smile and Reid felt his
body sway toward her.

A horn honked, startling him, and he jumped. He
blamed the long day behind the wheel for his preoc-
cupation with the pretty lady. He tore his gaze from
her brown eyes and watched his grandfather's jalopy
pull into a parking space. The ancient pickup should
have found its way to the junkyard a decade ago. This
wasn't how Reid imagined greeting his grandfather—
in the wee-morning hours—after returning to town all
these years.

The driver's-side door opened and Emmett Hardell
climbed out. A moment later Amelia Rinehart stepped
from the passenger side. What was his grandfather
doing at this late hour with the matriarch of Stampede?
He studied the pair—they'd both aged.

*That's what happens when you don't see people for
over a decade.*

"Good grief, Emmett." Amelia shut her door. "Riding in your truck is like lying on a magic fingers vi-
brating bed."

"What would you know about those kinds of beds?"
the old man grumbled.

"You'd be surprised by how many I've slept in," she
said.

The couple faced off unaware of their audience.
Amelia propped her fists on her hips and glared. "With
the income Paradise Ranch made during the holidays
you can afford to buy a new vehicle."

"Be a waste of good money—" he lifted his leg and
shook his foot "—when I got one boot in the grave already."

"You're too ornery to die." Amelia narrowed her eyes. "Speaking of ornery…when are you going to approve my idea to reinstate the Stampede Rodeo and Spring Festival?"

"Never."

"Why not?"

"Because every one of your bright ideas has cost me my privacy and peace of mind."

"What little mind you have left doesn't need any peace."

Ouch. Reid listened to the couple spar, wondering why they were awake let alone out together past their bedtimes.

"Don't worry," the blonde whispered. "Those two banter back and forth all the time. Gunner says they're in love and arguing is their version of foreplay."

His grandfather loved the old woman? Reid's grandmother had grown up with Amelia. The two women had been best friends most of their lives, but Emmett had never cared for the wealthy lady—at least not that Reid could remember. When Amelia had stopped by the ranch to check on the family after his grandma passed away, she'd always argued with Emmett.

"I should have introduced myself," she said to Reid. "I'm Scarlett Johnson and that lady is my great-aunt."

Scarlett Johnson. He hadn't recognized her. Reid had bumped into Scarlett at her great-uncle's funeral back when he'd been in high school. His looks must have changed, too, because she acted as if they'd never met.

"You're an old fuddy-duddy," Amelia said to Emmett. "I don't know why I ever thought you were a catch back in the day."

"You've messed with this town plenty," Emmett said. "Can't you leave it and me alone?"

"You enjoy me fussing over you," she said.

Emmett shook his head. "You should know better than to tie yourself to a corpse."

Amelia stamped her foot. "If you're so determined to die, hand over your shotgun and I'll put you out of your misery."

"You'd like that, wouldn't you," he said. "With me out of the way you'd turn Stampede into a three-ring circus."

"I better intervene before one of them gives the other a heart attack." Scarlett approached the couple. "Isn't it past your bedtimes?"

"We're too excited about the baby to sleep," Amelia said.

Emmett handed Scarlett a cell phone. "Gunner called and said he emailed photos of the baby, but I can't get into my phone."

Reid pulled his iPhone from his pocket and checked his text messages. Nothing—not that he'd expected his brother to share the happy news with him. He put the phone away and waited for the right moment to step out of the shadows.

"Emmett's phone is password protected and he forgot the password," Amelia said. "He thinks Gunner wrote it down on a sticky note and put in the office desk."

"He did," Scarlett said. "I saw the note. It said 'password.'"

Emmett nodded. "Good. Tell me what the password is."

"Password," Scarlett said.

"That's what I'm asking you." Emmett looked at Amelia. "Is your niece hard of hearing?"

Amelia shoved her elbow into Emmett's side. "The password is 'password,' you old fool."

"'Password'?" His grandfather harrumphed. "That's a stupid word for a password."

"Gunner assumed it would be easy for you to remember." Amelia spoke to her niece. "Lowercase?"

"Capital *P* and the rest is lowercase," Scarlett said.

Amelia's gaze landed on Reid. "I'm sorry. I didn't know you were helping a guest."

Like a man walking across wet cement, Reid dragged his feet forward. "Hey, Gramps."

The old man's eyes widened. "Reid?"

He smiled. "In the flesh."

"Reid Hardell?" Amelia narrowed her eyes. "Young man, it's about time you came home to visit your family."

"Yes, ma'am." His grandfather didn't crack a smile or offer a hug. Reid should have called before showing up out of the blue.

A shrill bark startled the group. Fang raced across the parking lot, his leash trailing behind him as Jessie tried to catch up. As soon as the dog saw Reid, he switched directions and ran over to him. Reid scooped the mutt into his arms.

"I wanted to try out the swings." Jessie stopped next to Reid and gasped for air. "But Fang took off." Her gaze zeroed in on Emmett's grumpy face. "Don't you like dogs?" When Emmett didn't answer her question, she said, "What's going on?"

"Jessie." Reid cleared his throat. "I'd like you to meet your great-grandfather."

Emmett's mouth sagged open. "This young'un is your daughter?"

Amelia smiled. "Emmett, you never told me that Reid had gotten married."

Reid handed Fang over to Jessie, then said, "I'm not married, Ms. Amelia."

"Jessie, come inside. Your dog looks like he needs a drink of water." Scarlett and his daughter entered the office, leaving Reid alone to face his grandfather.

"I should have warned you that I was coming," he said.

"You should have done a lot of things, young man." Emmett walked back to his truck and climbed behind the wheel, then stuck his head out the window. "Get in, Amelia. We're leaving."

The older woman clutched Reid's arm. "Don't mind his grumpiness. You just caught him by surprise. Come by my house tomorrow and talk to him."

"He's not living at the ranch?"

"Scarlett is staying in Emmett's room at the ranch and helping Sadie look after the twins until she finds an apartment." Amelia hopped into the pickup and waved out the window as his grandfather drove off.

Reid tore his gaze from the clunker and stared longingly at his own pickup. The temptation to leave Stampede was strong, but he'd stay and deal with the consequences of leaving the family fold.

He'd do it for Jessie.

And because he had nobody else to turn to.

REID'S DAUGHTER FILLED the plastic bowl with water from the cooler in the lobby, then set it on the floor for the dog. Once the little yapper drank his fill, she put him on a chair where he curled into a ball and closed his eyes.

"I like his Superman T-shirt," Scarlett said.

"Fang's always cold."

"Fang?"

"He lost one of his canine teeth." Jessie picked up a brochure advertising the petting zoo at Paradise Ranch. The young girl was slender with pretty blue eyes—like her father's.

Reid Hardell… Scarlett's thoughts skipped back to the day she'd attended her great-uncle's funeral in Stampede and had walked past the corner of the church and plowed into Reid, much the same way she had a few minutes ago. Only back then Reid had kissed her after he'd helped her up off the ground. Every summer when she and her cousins had visited Aunt Amelia, they'd been warned to stay away from *those wild Hardell boys* and now Lydia and Sadie were each married to one of them.

"How old are you?" Scarlett asked.

"Twelve." Jessie's gaze narrowed. "How old are you?"

"Twenty-eight." Wait until her cousins learned the middle brother was the father of a preteen daughter. "You and your dad arrived at an exciting time," she said. "My cousin Lydia is married to your uncle Gunner and she gave birth to a baby girl earlier this evening."

Jessie didn't comment, her pensive gaze shifting between the dog and her father in the parking lot. Scarlett's experience as a social worker insisted there was something off about the father-daughter relationship. "You and your dad will be staying in the *High Noon* room." She entered the code into the machine Gunner had taught her to use when she'd moved to town a few months ago.

"What's a high-noon room?" Jessie asked.

"Lydia helped your uncle renovate the motel last summer and instead of numbers on the room doors, she picked Western movie titles." Scarlett waved a hand. "The movies were way before your time."

Jessie's attention returned to the window. "What's there to do here?"

"Not much, but Paradise Ranch has a petting zoo, which might be busy next week when all the school kids are on spring break."

"I'm homeschooled."

This time Scarlett stared out the window. "Your father supervises your studies?"

Jessie shook her head. "My mom did, then Mrs. Valentine helped me. She's smart. She used to work at a bank."

"Who's Mrs. Valentine?"

"My foster mom."

Foster care. That explained the uneasiness between father and daughter.

Jessie sat next to Fang and the dog climbed into her lap. "My mom died."

"I'm so sorry, Jessie." Scarlett's heart swelled with compassion. "How long did you live with Mrs. Valentine?"

"Since September."

Six months. "I moved here from Wisconsin not that long ago. I'm a social worker in Mesquite."

"Mesquite?"

"A town about fifteen minutes from here."

"Mrs. Delgado's my caseworker. She's nice."

Scarlett wanted to know why the young girl had been put into foster care after her mother had died, but if she asked too many questions, Jessie might shut down.

"Fang belonged to Mrs. Valentine, but he liked me better, so she gave him to me." Jessie rubbed the mutt's head.

"When I was your age, I had a dog named Charlie," Scarlett said. "He slept with me in my bed."

"Fang sleeps with his head on my pillow. I wake up to dog breath in my face."

Scarlett laughed, then stopped abruptly when Reid entered the lobby. His hands were fisted at his sides and when his gaze landed on Jessie, the muscle in his jaw bunched. Scarlett had heard bits and pieces about Reid from her cousins but no one understood why the middle Hardell brother chose to keep his distance from the family. She'd always been a champion for the under-dog and hoped Reid and his brothers could make peace with the past.

"What's wrong?" Jessie asked.

"Nothing." He uncurled his fingers and looked at Scarlett. "Sorry about all the commotion. Jessie and I should have stopped at a motel in Mesquite or Rocky Point."

"She works in Mesquite." Jessie pointed to Scarlett.

Scarlett came out from behind the desk. "It's good that you stopped. Otherwise you wouldn't have heard about the baby." She spoke to Jessie. "Gunner and Lydia named their daughter Amelia after the older woman you saw in the parking lot." Her gaze swung between Reid and Jessie. "Me and my cousins are named after our great-grandmothers, but Aunt Amelia never had chil-dren, so Lydia and Gunner thought it would be nice to name their little girl after her."

Reid appeared unimpressed with the story. He rubbed his brow, drawing Scarlett's attention to the dark shadows beneath his eyes. "How far did you two drive to get here?"

"We came from El Paso," he said. "We got a late start."

El Paso? The last she'd heard Reid had been living in Albuquerque. "I'm sure you're ready to turn in for the night." Scarlett handed him a key card. "You'll be staying in the *High Noon* room."

At his raised eyebrow Jessie spoke. "The rooms are named after old movies."

He pulled out his wallet. "What do I owe you?"

"Nothing." Scarlett smiled. "You're family."

Reid grimaced as if she'd offended him, then put his wallet away.

"Need help with your luggage?" she asked.

"We'll be fine, thanks." He nodded to Jessie. "Grab the dog's supplies and your backpack. I'll bring the rest of our things."

Jessie carried Fang out of the office.

"If it's available," he said, "I'll need the room for a few days."

"You should stay at the ranch. I can move my things out of your grandfather's room."

"Why isn't my grandfather living at the ranch?" he asked.

"When I moved here, Aunt Amelia insisted Emmett stay with her while I searched for an apartment. I was only supposed to use your grandfather's room for a couple of weeks, but I've had so much fun with my cousin and nephews that I've been lazy about finding an apartment. Now that you're here I'll start looking again." She moved closer to Reid, catching a hint of woodsy aftershave. "I'm sure it would be okay if I moved my things into Gunner and Lydia's private room here at the motel."

"Private room?"

Scarlett nodded. "They made one of the rooms into a combination office and nursery in case Gunner ever brings the baby to work with him."

"I appreciate the offer, but I'd prefer a motel room for me and Jessie." He opened the lobby door, then motioned for her to precede him outside. "I should have asked first," he said, "are pets allowed?"

"They are." She pointed to the walkway between the rooms and the office. "There's a pet station stocked with plastic doggy doo-doo bags." Scarlett wanted to talk to Reid longer, but Jessie waited for him in front of their room.

Reid removed the suitcases from the back seat of the truck, then shut the door.

Before he walked off, she said, "You don't remember, do you?"

The corner of his mouth curved upward. "How could I forget? I cut my lip on your braces."

Her heart flipped on its end and twirled in a circle before dropping back into place. Reid Hardell remembered their kiss.

Scarlett's very *first* kiss.

"WHERE'S ELMO?" JESSIE dug through the bag of dog supplies in the motel room.

"It might be on the floor in the truck." Jessie had asked Reid to buy the dog toy after he'd insisted they take Fang to a vet before leaving El Paso. The visit to the walk-in animal clinic had delayed their departure and caused them to get stuck in Friday rush-hour traffic. The busy roads and having to shell out four hundred dollars for vaccinations and a year's worth of heartworm pills and flea-and-tick protection hadn't helped Reid's pensive mood.

Jessie filled Fang's water bowl. "Are you thirsty?" She spoke in a squeaky cartoon voice and the mutt's tail wagged so hard, he stumbled sideways, his front paw landing in the water bowl. After he finished drinking, Jessie picked him up and he licked her face. "Stop." She giggled. "That's gross."

Reid's chest tightened as he watched the pair. The only time he heard his daughter laugh was when Fang gave her kisses. During the six-month probation period where he and Jessie had gotten to know one another, he'd cracked a few jokes but they'd fallen flat. As for smiles… His daughter smiled—just not at him. That's why he'd been stunned when she'd answered *yes* after the social worker asked if she felt comfortable enough with Reid to live with him.

Jessie crawled into bed and Fang snuggled next to her, his bug eyes watching Reid unpack.

"Your grandfather isn't very nice," Jessie said.

"He's mad at me."

"Why?"

"I haven't been a very good grandson." He sat on the end of his bed and tugged off his boots.

"Why not?"

Reid didn't want his problems with his family to influence how Jessie got along with them. "Don't worry, my grandfather will come around." Gramps would never take his disappointment in Reid out on a defenseless kid.

"Scarlett's a social worker." Each time Jessie stroked

Fang's head, the dog's eyes closed for a second, then popped open.

"That's interesting." It was also interesting that whenever he'd looked into her brown eyes, he'd felt like he was being sucked into quicksand—a warm, soft quagmire.

"Scarlett seems nice."

Her doe-like eyes had hypnotized him all those years ago and without realizing what he was doing he'd started kissing her.

"Can you get my Kindle from my backpack?"

"Sure." Reid had learned after meeting Jessie that she didn't go anywhere without her electronic reading device. And according to Mrs. Delgado, his daughter was of above-average intelligence. After Stacy died, Jessie had been given the option to enroll in a public school but had declined, so the social worker had supervised her studies until Jessie had been placed in a foster home, where Mrs. Valentine took over the home-schooling duties.

Reid knew nothing about homeschooling and hadn't even been to college. He wasn't the right person to teach his daughter. They hadn't talked about Jessie attending a public school, but Reid didn't see any other option.

He retrieved the Kindle, then checked the clock on the nightstand. One o'clock. "You can read until I finish my shower, then lights out." He carried a clean pair of briefs and pajama bottoms into the bathroom and then stood under the hot spray, until the tension in his neck and shoulders eased. As his body relaxed, he focused his thoughts on Scarlett. He'd expected to encounter a few surprises returning home after all these years, but she hadn't been one of them. He'd thought Scarlett had been the prettiest girl he'd ever seen, and she'd only grown more beautiful since then. He grinned when he recalled bumbling their first and only kiss. He'd love to show her he'd learned a trick or two about kissing since then.

He turned off the water and stepped from the shower. After putting on his pj's, he ran the electric shaver over his face and erased his day-old beard. When he stepped from the bathroom, Jessie was sound asleep with the Kindle resting on her chest. He turned the gadget off and placed it on the nightstand.

His daughter was a tough girl. She kept things inside like he had at her age. Before he turned out the light, he studied her face, searching for traces of himself. Aside from her blue eyes and dark hair he couldn't see a resemblance. He hurt for Jessie. It was obvious she'd been close to her mother.

And now she's stuck with you.

But unlike his father who hadn't given a crap about him, Reid was determined that he'd always be there for Jessie as long as she needed him.

Chapter Two

Scarlett sipped her coffee in front of the hotel window as she watched the sun peek above the horizon Saturday morning.

She'd caught a few winks after Reid and Jessie had retired to their room last night, but she was eager to relinquish her desk duties to the part-time employee Gunner had hired to cover for him while he helped Lydia with the baby.

Her gaze swung to the *High Noon* room and she envisioned Reid sprawled across one of the double beds as he slept. The cowboy had been her first crush and she'd never forgotten him or his kiss. Every once in a while she'd recall that afternoon and wonder where he was or whom he was with. But she'd never imagined him being a father.

Eventually the streaks of pinkish orange along the horizon gave way to bright sunlight. The pace of life in Stampede was turtle slow compared to the hustle and bustle of Wisconsin's state capital. Last year she'd despised the tiny Texas town for luring her cousins away from Madison. Not in a million years had Scarlett believed she'd be living here, too.

If not for being duped by Dale, and having been

forced to resign from her job, she wouldn't have packed her belongings and moved south. Fortunately there was a need for social workers, and Family Crisis Services in Mesquite had offered her a job right away.

The door to the *High Noon* room opened and Jessie stepped outside with Fang. The little Chihuahua was dressed in his Superman T-shirt and his owner wore pajama bottoms, pink fuzzy slippers and a sweatshirt. Coffee in hand Scarlett left the office and followed the duo behind the motel. "Good morning," she said.

Jessie jumped, then slapped her hand against her chest. "Crap, you scared me."

"Sorry." Scarlett sat at the picnic table.

Jessie walked the dog until he did his job, then scooped him off the ground and joined Scarlett, placing Fang on top of the table.

"The plastic bags to pick up his doo-doo are over there." Scarlett pointed to the waste station.

Jessie put her hand in front of Fang's face and said, "Stay," then walked off to clean up the dog's mess. When she sat down again, she removed a single-serve can of pet food from the pocket of her sweatshirt and popped the lid off. Fang's tail twirled like a propeller as he gobbled his breakfast.

"Where did you get your coffee?" Jessie asked.

"There's a Keurig machine in the office. Do you drink coffee?"

The preteen nodded.

Twelve was a little young to get hooked on jitter juice. After the dog finished his meal, Scarlett said, "There's milk in the office fridge."

"I like coffee."

They returned to the office, where Jessie filled a

disposable cup with water from the cooler and offered Fang a drink.

"You take very good care of him." Scarlett watched Jessie make herself coffee, then dump three creamers and two packets of sugar into the cup—definitely not a proper breakfast for a twelve-year-old.

"If you like animals," Scarlett said, "then you'll love visiting the petting zoo at your great-grandfather's ranch."

Jessie sipped the hot brew, squinting over the rim of the cup. "If we're allowed to go to the ranch."

"What do you mean?"

"My dad said he wasn't a very good grandson."

Scarlett wondered how much of his childhood Reid had shared with his daughter.

"If no one wants my dad to stay, then we'll probably go back to El Paso."

Time to change the subject. "Are you hungry? There's a box of instant oatmeal in the back."

"Sure," Jessie said.

In the makeshift kitchen behind the office, Scarlett microwaved two bowls of apple-cinnamon oatmeal. When she handed Jessie her breakfast, the girl said, "You're really pretty."

"Thank you." Scarlett was aware of her beauty. She'd been blessed with flawless skin, luminous eyes and high cheekbones. As far as hairdos went, she looked good in any style, which was why she wore a wash-'n'-wear haircut, because it saved her time getting ready for work each morning.

"I used to have long hair." Scarlett touched her lower back. "All the way down to my hips. My friend told me guys liked long hair so I never cut it." She finished her oats. "Then I woke up one morning in college and stared at myself in the mirror and said, 'Why do I care what guys think?'" She smiled. "I cut it all off and I've been wearing it short ever since."

Jessie scratched Fang behind the ears and the dog's eyes closed. "My mom had long hair."

Scarlett sat down in a chair. "Were you and your mother close?"

Jessie nodded. "It was mostly just me and my mom."

"I was close to my mother when I was your age," Scarlett said.

"Is she still alive?"

"Yes. She taught second grade, but she's retired now."

"Do you have kids?"

"No."

"You don't want kids?"

"Someday maybe." Scarlett smiled to cover the sting she felt when she thought of Dale's daughter Amy. She'd loved the six-year-old as a mother not a social worker. "I have a full caseload of kids at work."

"My mom wanted more kids, but after Mike broke up with her, she never got another boyfriend."

Not only did Jessie have a rough time of it, but her mother had, too. "What kind of work did your mom do?"

"She was a supervisor in a warehouse."

"I like hearing about women bosses," Scarlett said.

Jessie sat up straighter. "Sometimes she drove a forklift."

"Impressive. The largest vehicle I've ever driven is the van I borrowed from a friend to move to a new apartment." Scarlett's cousins had nicknamed her *gypsy* because she only signed one-year leases at apartment complexes.

Jessie dropped her gaze. "My mom died at work."

Scarlett pictured a woman passing out at her desk after suffering a heart attack, stroke or brain aneurism. "What happened?"

"She backed the forklift into a bunch of wooden pallets and they fell on top of her."

Scarlett winced.

"My grandparents died a long time ago," Jessie said. "That's why Mrs. Delgado had to call my dad."

Had to call? "You didn't keep in touch with your father?"

Jessie shook her head. "My mom said he didn't want anything to do with us."

Wow. No wonder Reid and his daughter appeared uneasy with each other.

"His name was on my birth certificate." Jessie pulled Fang closer to her body as if the animal was a shield. "So I'm stuck with him."

Stuck? That wasn't the way things worked in social services, especially with children Jessie's age. If she hadn't wanted to be with Reid, her caseworker wouldn't have forced her to live with him.

The lobby door opened and Fang barked. Reid stepped inside, wearing pajama bottoms, a rumpled T-shirt, his cowboy boots and hat.

Scarlett smiled at the pillow crease along his cheek. "Good morning." It took immense willpower to maintain eye contact with him and not allow her gaze to drift over his muscular chest and the cotton bottoms clinging to his slim hips.

He dragged a hand down his tired face, then looked at his daughter. "I woke up and you weren't in the room."

"Fang had to pee," Jessie said.

"I bet you could use some caffeine." While Scarlett made him a cup of joe, a deafening silence filled the room. When she offered him the drink, his fingers skimmed her knuckles and tiny sparks raced up her arm. "There's cream and sugar on the table."

"Black is fine." He took a sip, then spoke. "You hungry?"

"We had oatmeal," Jessie said.

Scarlett smiled. "I can make you a bowl, if you'd like."

"I'll pass, thanks."

A vehicle pulling into the parking lot caught Scarlett's attention. "Sadie's here." She glanced at the wall clock. "She's up early."

The white minivan parked in front of the window and when the rear door opened, Scarlett's nephews hopped out and raced over to the office. It took both boys pulling on the handle to open the door and when they burst into the lobby, Tommy shouted, "Aunt Scarlett, we got a girl cousin!"

Scarlett laughed. "I heard."

"It sucks." Tommy looked at his brother. "Right, Tyler?"

Scarlett frowned at the pair. "Your mom told you not to use that word."

"I forgot." Tommy noticed Jessie sitting in the chair and walked over to her. "Is that your dog?"

"His name is Fang," Jessie said. "And just so you know, boys suck, too."

Tommy and Tyler exchanged wide-eyed glances.

"You two look alike," Jessie said.

"That's 'cause we're twins." Tommy nudged Tyler in the side. "Right?"

Tyler pointed to the dog. "Can I pet him?"

"Sure."

The boys took turns petting Fang and then Tommy spoke when Sadie walked into the office. "That's my mom."

Jessie pointed to Reid. "That's my dad."

"We've got two dads." Tommy glanced at Tyler and his brother nodded.

"Sadie, this is Reid." Scarlett introduced the adults. "And Reid's daughter, Jessie."

"You and Jessie couldn't have picked a better time to visit." Sadie smiled. "The whole family will be here when Lydia and Gunner bring the baby home from the hospital."

Scarlett loved her cousin for acting nonchalant about the fact that her husband's brother had returned to town unannounced and with a daughter no one had known about. Not that Sadie's easy-going personality put Reid at ease. His gaze swung to the door, then over to the window before returning to the door. The cowboy wanted to flee.

"Scarlett," Sadie said, "I need you to come with me and the boys to buy party supplies for the baby's homecoming tomorrow. I'm planning a surprise get-together for the new parents at the ranch." Sadie nodded to Jessie. "As long as the dog doesn't mind waiting in the van while we shop, why don't you come with us."

Tyler patted Jessie's thigh. "Will you come?"

Jessie looked at Reid, and he said, "We don't have any plans."

"Sure," Jessie said. "I'll go."

Reid's rigid stance relaxed. He didn't seem bothered that his daughter hadn't wanted to spend the day with him.

Jessie scooped Fang off the chair. "I'll get dressed."

"Do you have a key card to get back into the room?" Reid opened the lobby door for her after Jessie flashed the card in his face. "Take a twenty out of my wallet on the nightstand in case you see something you want to buy for yourself or the dog."

Sadie sent Scarlett a curious look when Jessie left without saying a word to anyone. "Boys, have you said hello to your dad's brother? This is your uncle Reid."

"I thought Uncle Gunner was Dad's brother," Tommy said.

"Your father has two brothers." Sadie smiled at Reid.

"Nice to meet you, boys," he said.

"We're five." Tommy walked over to Reid and squinted up at him. "My dad wears a cowboy hat but his is black."

Scarlett hid a smile behind a pretend yawn. The boy's forthrightness took getting used to.

"Are you older than my dad?" Tommy asked.

"Nope. I'm thirty-two." He studied the twins. "I can't tell you apart."

"That's 'cause we look alike," Tyler said.

Scarlett laughed. "You can tell them apart by remembering that Tommy asks a lot of questions and Tyler's favorite hobby is reading."

"Do you got more kids?" Tommy asked.

"No. Just my daughter, Jessie."

Tommy wrinkled his nose. "She's a girl."

Reid's mouth flirted with a smile and Scarlett was

mesmerized by the twinkle in his blue eyes. "Jessie's a girl all right."

"Is Fang a boy dog?" Tommy asked.

Reid nodded.

"Okay, enough questions." Sadie pointed across the room. "Pick out a book and read while we wait for Jessie."

Tyler walked over to the refurbished post office mailbox compartments and opened one of the doors. He removed a children's book from the slot, then climbed into a chair. Tommy sat next to his brother and listened to him read.

"When does Virginia take over for you?" Sadie asked Scarlett.

"Not until eight but Gunner said she usually shows up early." Scarlett turned to Reid. "Virginia lives across the street from our aunt."

Sadie laughed. "She's what Aunt Amelia calls a colorful character."

"Colorful is right," Scarlett said. "Virginia is pushing sixty, but dresses like a twenty-year-old."

Reid reached for the door handle. "Jessie's got my number in her cell phone if you need to get ahold of me."

"Before you go," Sadie said. "I have a message for you from Logan. Your brothers would like you to meet them at the Saddle Up Saloon at noon."

"Sure. Where should I pick up Jessie later?"

Sadie waved a hand. "Come out to the ranch. Jessie will enjoy helping the boys feed the petting-zoo animals."

"See you later then."

As soon as the door closed behind him, Sadie said, "He couldn't escape fast enough."

Scarlett watched Reid cross the parking lot. "I'd love to be a mouse in the bar when the Hardell brothers meet later."

"Let's make a list of party supplies while we wait for Virginia to arrive."

Scarlett retrieved a notepad and a pen from the desk drawer, eager to hear how Sadie planned to decorate for both the baby and the black sheep's homecoming.

REID PARKED THE pickup behind the old Woolworth building in downtown Stampede. It was five minutes before noon and his gut was tied into a pretzel knot.

The Hardell family reunion would be a far cry from a Hallmark movie scene. He'd be lucky if he escaped the gathering with his surname intact.

He got out of the truck and strolled along the town's main thoroughfare—Chuck Wagon Drive. A handful of brick buildings dated back to the late 1800s and early 1900s. The feed store had closed its doors and boarded over the windows before Reid had graduated from high school. He could barely make out the words For Sale that had been spray-painted on the side of the building decades ago.

His gaze swung across the street. The old Amoco filling station had been converted into a farmer's market. A pickup was parked in the lot, its truck bed piled high with produce. Next to the station sat the Corner Market. When he was a kid, his grandfather would drop him and his brothers off at the store to buy candy.

He continued up the next block. The town looked depressed. Tired. The white bench that had always sat in front of the National Bank and Trust was missing and weeds grew through the cracks in the sidewalk near the door. On the other side of the street the shadows of the missing letters in the Bucket of Suds Coin-Operated Laundry sign remained visible against the gray cinder block.

From the few texts he'd exchanged with his brothers over the last year he knew his grandfather was trying to sabotage Amelia's efforts to restore the town—he just didn't know why. He agreed with the matriarch that the place needed a face-lift. If she wanted to dump her millions into Stampede, why should his grandfather care?

Reid put the brakes on and backpedaled to Millie's Antiques & Resale—or what used to be the business. The old rocker that had sat in the display window for decades had been replaced with an industrial-style desk and a hanging light made from plumbing pipes and old-fashioned Edison light bulbs. *Lydia's Interior Design* was etched into the window glass.

Gunner hadn't told him that his wife had opened a business in town. The canary yellow door and red flowerpots overflowing with white and purple pansies was the lone bright spot among the dreary buildings on the block.

Reid reached the Saddle Up Saloon and drew in a steadying breath. Then another. And another. But no amount of oxygen would clear his thinking enough to fabricate a reasonable excuse for ignoring his family all these years.

He entered the building, pausing inside the door to allow his eyes to adjust to the dim interior. He looked toward the bar expecting to see his brothers parked on the stools, but the seats were empty.

Reid recognized the bartender dusting off liquor

bottles. JB's ponytail was longer and mostly gray now. He wore a beige T-shirt with a picture of a saddle on the back and the bar name printed in bold, black letters. When JB recognized Reid, the corner of his mouth lifted in greeting, then he tilted his head toward a table in the back corner where his siblings and his grandfather had gathered.

Reid approached the group and waited for an invite to join them. His grandfather nodded and Reid pulled out a chair and sat. JB placed a bottle of beer in front of Reid, then refilled his grandfather's coffee cup before returning behind the bar.

He might as well get the tongue-lashing over with. Staring at his older brother he said, "Give me your best shot."

Logan didn't hesitate. "You've treated us like lepers for years. Don't think you can waltz back into the family as if you never left."

"I doubt you missed me that much," Reid muttered.

Logan's eyes widened.

"I'm no saint." Gunner spoke up. "I've done my share of letting everyone down, but I've never deserted the family." He pointed to their grandfather. "Gramps took care of us when our parents didn't. He deserved better from you."

Reid stared at his grandfather and braced himself.

"Did I do something or say something to make you believe you weren't part of this family?"

Reid clenched his jaw and looked away from the sadness in the old man's eyes. "I'd rather not talk about the past." What good would it do to list his grievances? Donny Hardell was dead and his brothers had moved on. Why couldn't he?

"Why'd you come home?" Gunner asked.

Tell them the truth. "I didn't know where else to go for help."

"You having some kind of early-life crisis, boy?" Gramps asked.

Reid pressed his lips together to keep from smiling. Despite his belief that his brothers could have done more to protect him from their father's verbal abuse, he'd missed his grandfather's cantankerous personality. "If you consider instant fatherhood an early-life crisis, then yes, I'm having one."

Gunner looked at Logan, then back at Reid. "What do you mean, 'instant fatherhood'?"

"I met Jessie for the first time six months ago when social services contacted me after her mother died."

"The girl's mother is dead?" Gramps asked.

"Stacy died in a workplace accident. My name was listed on Jessie's birth certificate. A DNA test confirmed that I'm her father."

Gramps sipped his coffee. "Where's Jessie been all this time?"

"El Paso." Reid rubbed his brow. He'd never learn why Stacy hadn't reached out to him after she discovered she was pregnant. Her reasons had been cremated along with her body.

"I don't remember any Stacy that we went to school with," Logan said.

"She wasn't from here."

"Where did she live?" Gunner asked.

"I don't know. The subject never came up at Jason Zelder's house party where we had sex. Once." Stacy had latched onto Reid when he'd walked through the front door and hadn't let go until after they'd made out in his grandfather's pickup in the driveway. "Stacy left the party with her friends and I never heard from her again."

Gramps thumped his fist on the tabletop and they all jumped. "Why'd you wait six months to tell me about my great-granddaughter?"

"I wasn't sure Jessie wanted anything to do with me."

"What do you mean?" Gramps asked.

"The social worker suggested a six-month probation period for us to get to know each other. I quit my job in Albuquerque and moved to El Paso. At the end of six months Jessie agreed to leave her foster parents' home and go with me."

"So you got custody of her," Gunner said.

"Temporary custody. The caseworker will reevaluate our situation in the next couple of months and either recommend that a judge give me permanent custody or place Jessie back into the foster-care system." If he wanted to keep his daughter with him, Reid had to provide Jessie with a stable home life and a decent place to live. Right now they had neither of those things.

Logan crossed his arms over his chest. "I'm surprised you'd want anything to do with your daughter after the way you wrote off your family."

Reid's knuckles turned white against the beer bottle. "I think it's the other way around."

Their grandfather sliced his hand through the air, ending the tit for tat before it escalated. "How do you plan to show the social worker that Jessie belongs with us?"

He shrugged. "I don't know the first thing about being a father." And growing up, his father hadn't been a good role model.

"I won't be any help. As a first-time daddy I'm flying by the seat of my jeans." Gunner nudged Logan's arm. "You've been a father longer than I have."

"Only by a few months," Logan said. "I love the twins as if they were my own, but they're a lot younger than Jessie. And they're boys. I wouldn't know what to do with a preteen daughter."

"I got plenty of experience riding herd over teenage troublemakers," Gramps said. "How long are you staying?"

"If I can find a job and a place for Jessie and I to live, then we'll stay until the social worker makes her decision."

"What about school?" Logan asked.

"Jessie's mother and foster mother homeschooled her. I don't know anything about that stuff, so she'll have to go to the middle school in Mesquite."

"We can make room for you two at the ranch," Gramps said.

Logan raised his hand. "I need to check with Sadie first to see if it's okay with two more people moving into the house."

Reid didn't want to add stress to his brother's marriage and he didn't want to kick Scarlett out of his grandfather's bedroom. "If you can put Jessie up at the house, I'll stay at the motel." He nodded to Gunner. "I'll pay for the room."

"How are you supposed to bond with your daughter if you're not living together?" Gramps asked.

"It's only temporary," Reid said. "Once I find a job, I'll rent an apartment." Living a few miles away from his family would give him a little breathing room.

"You've finally come home after all these years," his

grandfather said. "I won't have you living in another town." He rubbed the whiskers on his chin. "What about bunking down in the old hunting cabin at the back of the property?"

"I appreciate the thought, Gramps," Reid said. "But it might be easier—" and less stress on the entire family "—if we find an apartment."

"If you want our help," Gramps said, "then you and Jessie should live at the ranch."

Reid liked the idea of Jessie being closer to family and if they used the cabin, he'd be closer to Scarlett, who he hadn't stopped thinking about since yesterday. And suddenly the thought of running into Scarlett on a regular basis appealed to Reid.

"What do you say?" Gramps said. "The cabin needs a good cleaning, but Jessie would have her own bedroom."

"Sure. We'll give it a try."

Logan hadn't said a word and Reid suspected his brother wasn't thrilled with the living arrangements.

Gramps changed the subject. "Gunner, what time are you bringing Lydia and the baby home from the hospital tomorrow?"

"At noon," Gunner said. "Why?"

"Stop by the ranch on your way into town. The women are cooking up a surprise party for the baby."

"You weren't supposed to tell Gunner," Logan said.

Their grandfather scoffed. "Men don't care about parties."

"I need to get back to the hospital." Gunner stood and pushed his chair in. "Thanks again for the car seat, Logan. It was easy to install." Gunner turned to Reid. "Welcome home."

After the youngest Hardell departed, Logan stood. "I've got to get back to the ranch. A group of trail riders arrives in a couple of hours."

Reid wanted to learn more about the changes at the ranch but kept his questions to himself. If he and Jessie were moving into the cabin, he'd find out soon enough why a cattle ranch had been turned into a tourist attraction.

Logan placed his cowboy hat on his head. "You leaving or staying, Gramps?"

"I got a meeting with the town council at the library."

"Town council?" Reid looked at his grandfather.

"Gramps is the mayor of Stampede," Logan said. "You would know that if you'd come home before now." He walked out of the bar.

"Don't mind your brother. He's a Hardell. We're all too stubborn for our own good."

Reid swallowed his pride. "I'm sorry."

"Growing up in this family wasn't easy. I know that." His grandfather braced his hands on the table and pushed himself to his feet. "You don't have to like any of us, but family is family and we're all you've got."

Reid sat alone in the saloon long after his *family* had deserted him. *Again*. Gramps and Gunner had been more forgiving than Logan. Reid had some fence mending to do with his older brother.

Chapter Three

"We've been waiting for you, Reid," Jessie said after he pulled up to the house at Paradise Ranch Saturday afternoon. "Scarlett's gonna give us a tour of the petting zoo."

In the six months that they'd known each other, Jessie hadn't called him *Dad*, even though she referred to him as *her dad* when she spoke with other people. Maybe she just needed a little more time.

He studied his childhood home. His grandmother's rosebushes looked healthy and lush—a big change from his last glimpse of the sickly shrubs as he'd left for the military. Fresh gravel covered the road leading to the highway and the swing hung on the porch again. The window trim had recently been painted and the white rockers were new. He attributed the homey feel to Logan's wife, Sadie.

"What's the matter?" Jessie asked.

"Nothing." He cracked a smile. "I haven't been here in a while and the place looks different." The barn sported a new coat of red paint and the white corral rails gleamed in the sun. Across from the old storage shed was an enclosed barnyard where a handful of animals congregated. A sign reading Paradise Petting Zoo hung above the entrance.

"You're here." Scarlett joined Jessie on the porch. Her smile reached her eyes, and the sparkle warmed his insides. He'd desired his share of women through the years and he felt plenty of below-the-belt temptation for Scarlett, but when their gazes locked all that heat traveled upward into his chest, making his heart pound faster.

Jessie descended the steps. "Uncle Logan said he had to take care of the horses."

A bitter lump lodged in Reid's throat when Jessie referred to his brother as *Uncle* Logan. Returning to Stampede was supposed to help *him* and Jessie grow closer, not Jessie and his brothers.

Tommy flung the front door open and he and his brother raced past Scarlett. "I want to show Jessie my chicken."

"Me, too," Tyler said.

Taking a look at the hunting cabin would have to wait until after they toured the barnyard. "Lead the way," he said.

The twins grabbed Jessie's hands, then Tommy said, "C'mon, JJ. I'll show you Captain America."

"And Superman," Tyler said. The boys and Jessie cut across the yard.

Scarlett descended the steps and they followed the kids. *"JJ?"* he said.

"Tommy kept complaining that Jessie was a girl, so she told the boys to call her JJ for short because it sounded like a boy's nickname." Scarlett peeked up at him. "What's the second *J* stand for?"

"Jones." He lowered his voice. "We haven't talked about changing her last name to Hardell." He figured his daughter needed time to get used to the idea of him being her father.

"Maybe she's waiting for a signal from you that you want her to take your surname." Was Scarlett speaking as a friend or a social worker?

"Jessie said the two of you didn't meet until after her mother died."

He didn't want to talk about Stacy—mostly because he felt bad that he couldn't remember much about her.

Scarlett pulled on his shirtsleeve and they stopped walking. "I'm prying because I care." She glanced ahead at the kids. "I've helped hundreds of girls like Jessie. I'm here if you have any questions or just want to talk."

Coming from anyone other than a social worker, Reid would have ignored the person, but Scarlett's offer was sincere and empathy shone in her brown eyes. "Thanks."

A wrinkle appeared across her brow. "It can be challenging bonding with a child you don't know well."

He almost asked if she had any tips on setting boundaries for a twelve-year-old but changed his mind, not wanting to appear totally inept as a parent. They strolled through the empty barn, then walked out the rear door into the petting corral.

"Watch this, JJ." Tommy chased a rooster whose comb looked as if it weighed more than the bird.

"Superman's hungry." Tyler pushed the button on the feeding machine attached to the corral rail and pellets spilled into his hands and onto the ground. He offered the treats to the goat and giggled when the animal licked his palm. "He likes his magic food."

"That's a weird-looking chicken." Jessie pointed to a

bird with a feather duster attached to its back end. "The tail is longer than its body."

"That's an Onagadori chicken. It was first bred in Japan," Scarlett said. "I didn't know a thing about chickens before I came to visit, but thanks to Tyler's chicken-and-rooster books I'm an expert." She patted a miniature horse. "This is Ruby."

"We got Ruby from a newspaper," Tyler said.

Jessie rubbed the mare's nose. "What do you mean, you got her from a newspaper?"

"Ruby's owner couldn't take care of her," Sadie said. "He put an ad in the newspaper, hoping someone would adopt her."

"Our grandpa lets us ride her." Tommy took Jessie's hand. "Wanna see Wilbur?" They zigzagged between chickens and stopped in front of a doghouse. "Come out, Wilbur." A pink snout appeared in opening.

Jessie knelt down. "Come out and play, piggy."

Tyler squatted by his brother and grunted like a pig. Wilbur left his house and nudged Jessie's hand with his nose. Her laughter warmed Reid's heart.

"The twins have a new best friend." Scarlett nodded to Jessie. "I hope they don't annoy her too much."

Reid watched the trio play with Wilbur. His family had accepted Jessie into their fold. Time would tell if they rolled out the welcome mat for him.

"How long did you plan to stay in Stampede?" Scarlett asked.

Apparently no one expected him to stick around.

What else are they supposed to believe when you've kept your distance all these years?

"I don't have any intention of leaving soon," he said.

"Jessie and I are moving into the cabin on the other side of the property."

"You don't sound excited about bunking down out there," she said. "My offer to stay at the motel still stands."

"The cabin will be fine." He wasn't pushing Scarlett out of the house. He needed an ally close by. He hoped he and his family could move forward because his daughter was making herself at home on the ranch and if they had to leave, she'd blame him for things not working out.

"Aunt Scarlett?" Tyler patted Scarlett's leg. "Can we show Jessie our tree house?"

"Check with your mom first." Scarlett glanced at Reid. "Logan built the boys a tree fort not too far from the garden alongside the house."

"Jessie, keep an eye on the boys," Reid said.

"I will." She followed the twins out of the barnyard and across the lawn to the back door of the house.

"When did you plan to look at the cabin?" Scarlett asked.

"Right now. You want to come along?" He winced at the eager note in his voice. He was still bruised from the dressing-down his brothers had given him earlier and it was nice to be with someone he didn't have to keep his guard up with.

"I don't have Lydia's eye for interior design or Sadie's talents in the kitchen and garden, but I know what girls Jessie's age like and don't like." They left the corral and Scarlett secured the latch on the gate. "I'll tell Sadie where we're going and meet you out front."

Reid walked back to his truck and listened to the radio while he waited for Scarlett. He drummed his fingers against the steering wheel to the beat of the music and gazed out the windshield. As a kid he'd raced down the gravel road to the highway hundreds of times to catch the school bus. He thought he'd never return after he'd caught the bus that had taken him to boot camp. Life sure had a way of turning the best-laid plans upside down and inside out.

"WHERE'S EMMETT?" SCARLETT asked when she entered the kitchen.

"Upstairs changing clothes." Sadie poured dish soap into the sink and ran the water. "Fang raced through the room a few minutes ago and tripped Emmett. When he caught himself on the counter, he tipped the bowl of cake batter onto his pants and shirt." Sadie pointed to the mess on the floor.

"I'd help clean up, but Reid's waiting for me in the driveway." Scarlett stepped over the splatter. "We're going to check out the cabin he and Jessie are staying in."

"I don't know why Gunner and Logan suggested the cabin." Sadie shut off the water. "It's silly to have them living on the other side of the ranch away from the rest of us."

"I think you need to let the guys figure out the logistics." Scarlett went into the laundry room and grabbed a small cooler from the shelf above the dryer.

Sadie followed her. "Are you telling me to mind my own business?"

"I wouldn't do that."

Sadie laughed. "Yes, you would."

"You're a mom and you like to fix everyone's problems."

"That's the pot calling the kettle black," Sadie said. "You've made a career out of fixing kids' problems."

"And my professional opinion is that it's important for Jessie and Reid to have their privacy while they get to know each other better." She returned to the kitchen and removed two bottles of water from the fridge, then put a handful of grapes into a plastic baggie.

"What are you doing?"

"Packing a picnic lunch." Scarlett ignored Sadie's arched eyebrow. She'd never told her cousins that Reid had kissed her the day of their great-uncle's funeral or that he'd crossed her mind through the years and even more often after her cousins had married his brothers.

"Are you treating this trip to the cabin like one of your family welfare visits?" Sadie asked.

"If I said no, would you drop the subject?"

Sadie's eyes twinkled. "Yes."

"Then, no."

Sadie went back to the sink and began wiping up the cake splatter. Scarlett knew her cousin had stopped her interrogation because she was glad Scarlett was showing interest in a man. After her horrible breakup with Dale, Scarlett had refused to get back into the dating game. Her cousins had suggested an online dating site, but she hadn't been ready. Now she wondered if she'd been ready all along but just waiting for the right guy—a guy like Reid.

"There's leftover chicken salad in the crisper," Sadie said.

"Good idea." Scarlett dished a scoop into two plastic bowls, then covered them and tossed in a pair of plastic forks. "I've got my cell," she said. "Call if anything comes up with the kids."

"We'll be fine."

Sadie followed Scarlett to the front door. "What about supper? Emmett's making fried chicken and Aunt Amelia is joining us. Should I plan on Jessie and Reid, too?"

"I'll let him know that everyone expects him for dinner." Scarlett hugged Sadie. "After the kids go to bed tonight, I'll help blow up the balloons." She stepped outside and closed the door preventing Sadie from following her onto the porch.

"What's that?" Reid asked when Scarlett set the cooler on the floor and climbed into the passenger seat.

"A snack if we get hungry."

Reid shifted the pickup into Drive and took off. "We can get to the cabin faster using the highway," he said.

"I didn't know there was another way to get there."

He nodded. "A couple of dirt roads intersect the ranch, but I don't know what shape they're in."

Scarlett stared at the passing scenery. "Texas is so different from Wisconsin. I'm used to cornfields and bean fields. Down here all you see is hay or cattle."

"Do you like the winters up north?" he asked.

"I enjoy the different seasons but the older I grow, the less I like the cold. We got a lot of snow this past winter and there were a few days I couldn't drive in to work."

A commercial came on the radio and when they both reached to turn the volume down at the same time, their fingers bumped. Scarlett looked away first because she didn't want him to see her blush like a schoolgirl. "Sadie and Lydia mentioned you settled in Albuquerque. How'd you end up there?"

"I landed a job as a mechanic for a trucking company." He slowed the pickup and moved over to the shoulder, then turned onto the property. "It looks like my grandfather had fresh gravel put down on this road, too."

Scarlett sensed Reid didn't want to talk about his life in New Mexico so she dropped the subject. "I can't believe my cousins married your brothers after my great-aunt warned us girls to steer clear of you boys."

"Amelia was right to be concerned about Gunner and Logan, but not me."

She laughed. "Maybe I imagined it was you who kissed me at the church that day."

He grinned. "That was pretty bold, huh?"

"You were my first kiss."

He glanced at her. "No way."

"Yes way."

"The guys in Wisconsin must have been dumber than the dairy cows up there not to try to steal a kiss from a girl as pretty as you."

She laughed. "Watch what you say about our cows."

The next time Reid glanced across the seat, his eyes dropped to her mouth. "I'm a better kisser now."

Scarlett's pulse kicked into overdrive and the temperature inside the cab inched higher. "Just so you know, I'm a better kisser, too."

"I'll take that as a challenge."

"You should." She turned her face toward the window. She didn't know if she was more shocked at herself for sparring with Reid or for enjoying it so much.

"Where'd you go to college?" he asked.

"University of Wisconsin at Madison. I wanted to go out of state but my parents said it was too expensive."

"Are your folks still in Madison?"

"Yes, but they're making plans to move to Florida.

Sadie's parents bought a home down there and Mom and Dad fell in the love with the retirement community. Dad's a computer geek and he can work anywhere. Mom retired from teaching a few years ago, so they're ready for a change."

"Brothers or sisters?" he asked.

"Sadie, Lydia and I are only children." Reid parked the truck in front of the cabin and she said, "It could use some paint." They got out and walked closer.

Cedar trees surrounded the small structure made from shiplap. The corrugated metal roof was rusted but gave the place a charming country feel. Two wooden poles and a crossbeam held up the overhang. "A couple of chairs on the porch would welcome visitors." Her eyes strayed to the dense foliage surrounding the cabin.

"What's the matter?" he asked.

"I'm checking for serial killers lurking in the woods."

He chuckled. "You think Jessie might object to sleeping this far away from the main house?"

"I don't know. But it wouldn't hurt to clear away some of the brush to allow more sunshine in."

"Let's take a look inside." He opened the door. "You might want to wait a minute and let me check for any furry squatters."

"Good idea." She backed up a step.

Reid left the door open and she heard his boots clomp against the plank floor. A minute later he called out. "All clear."

She entered the cabin expecting the worst, but was pleasantly surprised. Years of dust and dirt clung to the walls and floor—but nothing a good scrubbing wouldn't take care of. "Is there a bathroom?"

He pointed down a short hallway and Scarlett poked

her head inside. Sparse but functional. There were two small bedrooms, each with a window. "Electricity?"

Reid flipped a switch on the wall and the overhead light above the kitchen sink came on. That answered her question.

"When is Jessie's social worker doing a home visit?" It wasn't any of Scarlett's business but it was difficult to not voice questions she'd been trained to ask.

"Mrs. Delgado is supposed to call next week." He spread his arms wide. "We need furniture."

"There's a resale shop in Mesquite," she said. It was near the social service's office.

"Maybe I should look for a furnished apartment."

"I think Jessie needs family by her while you two…" Scarlett snapped her mouth closed.

"I guess the awkwardness between Jessie and me is obvious."

Scarlett's heart swelled with affection for Reid—a fondness that she told herself had nothing to do with the way his blue-eyed gaze roamed over her face, stalling on her mouth before looking away.

She touched his arm, hoping to reassure him. "It'll take time for her to trust you."

"I was seeing her twice a week for six months. How much time does she need?"

"You haven't been in her life for twelve years." When he expelled a heavy breath she said, "You can't just insist she can trust you. Promises mean nothing to her right now. You have to show Jessie. Every day she sees that you're still here, she'll begin to believe that you're not going to leave."

"This situation isn't my fault." He shoved a hand

through his hair. "Stacy never contacted me after she found out she was pregnant."

"What did Stacy tell Jessie about you?"

"I have no idea. I didn't ask."

"You need to talk with her. You don't want any misunderstandings between you."

"If my daughter didn't think I cared, she wouldn't have agreed to leave her foster home and live with me."

"You'd be surprised the decisions kids make because they yearn to be loved." She offered a reassuring smile. "You two will be fine."

"Maybe this wasn't such a good idea," he said.

"What?"

"Coming back to Stampede."

Scarlett's heart sank. The last thing she'd meant to do was discourage Reid from staying in town, especially when he hadn't been home in over a decade. "You can't leave." She winced at the eager note in her voice. "Being with family will play in your favor when the social worker decides whether or not you should be given permanent custody of Jessie."

"Got any other reasons why I shouldn't leave?"

She shook her head. "That's it, why?"

His mouth curved into a smile. "I thought maybe you'd want to judge for yourself if my kissing has improved."

"Well, there is that, too." Scarlett smiled. "But first, I'm hungry." If the warmth in his eyes was any indication, Reid was hungry, too—but not for food. He followed her out to the porch and they sat on the step, the cooler resting between them. She handed him the chicken salad and a fork.

He finished the snack, then looked at her hands.

"You're pretty and smart. Why hasn't some lucky guy put a ring on your finger yet?"

"I had a ring on that finger once." *Darn.* Why had she brought up her failed relationship?

His gaze locked with hers. "What happened?"

"Turns out he didn't love me after all."

"His loss."

Dale had doted on Scarlett as if she'd walked on water. Once she'd testified on his behalf in court and he'd won full custody of his daughter, suddenly Scarlett wasn't what he and Amy needed after all.

"I appreciate the vote of confidence," she said. "But social workers tend to view the glass half empty."

"It's understandable with everything you see in your job," he said.

"I went into this line of work believing I could change the world and champion children." She'd shed a lot of tears when she'd learned that she couldn't always protect the children in her care, never mind protect herself from having her heart broken.

"Why do you stay in the job?"

"Because I want to help kids. I want to make their world a little better." No more career talk. "What about you?" she asked. "Was there ever a special woman in your life?"

"No steady girlfriends while I was in the marines."

"And after you settled in Albuquerque?"

"I dated a woman for a few months, but it didn't work out."

"Do you think you'd like to get married someday?"

"I don't know that a few good years is worth the pain that comes afterward."

"You're talking about your parents," she said.

"How much do you know about their relationship?"

"Lydia and Sadie said your father was fast and loose with the buckle bunnies and that he wasn't at home much when you and your brothers were growing up."

"Did they tell you about my mother?"

"When she had enough of your dad's cheating, she abandoned the family," Scarlett said.

"My mother was no saint. She'd take off with her girlfriends for days at a time when my father wasn't home."

"Parents aren't perfect, but we shouldn't let them define who we want to be and what we want out of life."

"You're speaking from experience?"

"My parents were disappointed when I chose to go into social work. They wanted me to pick a career where I'd make more money. But helping children is my passion." She nudged his arm. "What's your passion?"

He turned his hands over and spread his fingers wide. "Working with these. I've always enjoyed fixing engines. The military taught me more about engines than I would have picked up in trade school. I'm no technology expert but I learned how to use computer programs to diagnose engine problems." He smiled. "I can make an honest living with my hands, but I'll never be wealthy."

"Money is overrated."

He chuckled. "Have you told your parents that?"

"Heavens no. They're on my case all the time to change professions, but I'd rather do what I love."

His blue eyes darkened. "I really like you, Scarlett."

Reid's declaration wasn't swoon-worthy but for a

woman who dealt with the ugly side of life on a daily basis, it was a beacon of sunshine filled with hope and possibilities.

Chapter Four

"Emmett, you've outdone yourself with this fried chicken." Amelia licked her fingers.

The old man grunted. "You're just saying that to butter me up."

"I am not," Amelia insisted.

"Are, too."

Fang raced around the table, stopping next to Tommy's chair when a piece of chicken dropped on to the floor.

"Tommy, I told you not to feed the dog," Sadie said. "I don't want him throwing up on the carpet later."

"He won't puke." Jessie waved her fork in the air. "Mr. Valentine let Fang eat out of the garbage can and he never got sick."

"Maybe you should tie Fang up on the back porch during supper," Reid said, wanting to avoid a family argument.

Jessie shoved her chair back, swooped Fang into her arms and left the room. When she returned, she said, "Don't blame me if he poops on the porch. He doesn't like to be alone."

Conversation resumed—Tommy doing most of the talking. The kid reminded Reid of a much younger

Logan, who'd talked nonstop at the supper table. His big brother had always been the last one to finish his meal.

Reid felt a gentle tap against the top of his shoe and looked at Scarlett sitting across from him. Her eyes sparkled with humor as if she'd guessed his thoughts. He'd known her less than twenty-four hours but his gut insisted she was the kind of person who gave people the benefit of the doubt and tried to find a little bit of good in everyone, despite her job where she saw the ugly side of human nature.

"Gramps double-fries his chicken. That's what makes it so good." Gunner made a loud smacking noise that the twins tried to imitate.

"If a little extra grease would make you listen to reason," Amelia said, "I'd dump a gallon of lard on your head."

Logan and Gunner chuckled, then coughed behind their napkins when Gramps shot them a dirty look.

Amelia's knobby finger signaled out each person at the table. "Everyone in this room believes bringing back the rodeo and festival will increase business for the motel, the trail rides and the petting zoo." The old woman narrowed her gaze on the eldest Hardell brother. "Logan, your grandfather says I should leave this town alone so it can wither up and die."

"Gramps has never been a progressive," Logan said.

"There's nothing wrong with Stampede the way it is," their grandfather grumped.

"There's no one left but old people," Amelia argued. "If younger families don't settle here, this place will turn into a ghost town."

"All the better," Gramps said.

"Your grandfather is an old fuddy-duddy," Amelia said. "You boys have known that for long time."

"Can't you wait until I die to spit-shine the place?"

"Here we go again." Amelia rolled her eyes—a gesture the older woman performed often in his grandfather's presence. "He talks as if he's on death's door."

Emmett glared.

Amelia ignored him and spoke to the rest of the family. "We need the festival to draw people to this town so they can see for themselves that it's a great place to raise a family. Everyone loves a rodeo celebration."

"It's a nice idea, Amelia, but I've got my hands full running the petting zoo and giving trail rides." Logan's gaze swung to Gunner.

"Don't look at me. I just had a baby."

The twins giggled. "No you didn't, Uncle Gunner," Tyler said. "Aunt Lydia had a baby."

"Fine. Lydia had the baby, but I'm busy with the motel."

"I don't want a bunch of strangers invading this town and littering everywhere," Emmett grumbled.

"I don't mind picking up trash as long as they leave their money behind," Amelia said.

"Reid doesn't have a job right now," Logan said. "Maybe he has time to help organize the event."

Figures his brother would throw him under the bus.

Amelia's face lit up. "That's a wonderful idea."

"I don't have any experience with organizing anything," Reid said. "And I'll be busy cleaning the cabin."

"Is it dirty?" Jessie asked. "'Cause if it's gross, I don't want to live there."

"It'll be fine for a short while."

"Short while?" Jessie looked over the top of Tommy's head at Reid. "I thought you said we were moving here."

Reid had used the word *move* when he and his daughter had discussed returning to Stampede, but in his mind he'd meant that he intended to test the waters with his family before making a final decision. "Staying depends on whether or not I find a job."

Tommy tugged on Jessie's sleeve. "You and Fang can live here with us."

"Thought you didn't like girls," Emmett said.

"I don't." Tommy shrugged. "But JJ likes our tree house and she's not afraid of Wilbur."

"And she likes to read." Tyler gazed at Jessie with hero worship in his eyes. "Right, JJ?"

Jessie nodded.

"I think Jessie should stay in the house until the cabin is ready," Sadie said. "If you don't mind sleeping on the couch, you can use my office as your bedroom."

"I slept on a couch when I lived with my mom," Jessie said.

Reid wished his daughter hadn't mentioned her mother. His family had questions about Stacy—questions he didn't know the answers to. He looked at Jessie. "If you want, you can help me clean the cabin tomorrow."

"No, thanks." She shoveled a bite of food into her mouth, unaware that rejecting her father's offer had surprised her relatives.

"Back to the rodeo and festival," Amelia said. "Sadie, you're already taking care of the ranch books, so you'll be in charge of making sure the bills get paid and we have the proper permits and insurance."

Why wasn't Logan taking care of the ranch finances?

And what had his brother been doing with the thousand dollars Reid sent home every month?

"Logan, I want you and Gunner to call your cowboy friends and make sure they put the rodeo on their schedules. And I expect all three of you boys—" Amelia's gaze pinged off each Hardell brother "—to compete in the rodeo."

Logan removed a pen and notebook from his shirt pocket and jotted down Amelia's instructions. "When's the rodeo?"

"The second weekend in April."

"That's only a month away," Sadie said.

Amelia ignored Emmett's snicker. "Plenty of time,"

"Gunner, you and Lydia can be in charge of advertising and promotion."

"I'm sure she'll be thrilled to hear that, when I pick her and the baby up from the hospital tomorrow," Gunner grumbled.

Amelia's gaze swung to Reid. "You're in charge of the rodeo. As I've told my nieces time and time again, there is no budget. I want you to hire a well-respected stock contractor."

"Are there gonna be carnival rides?" Jessie asked.

"I hadn't considered rides, young lady, but that's a brilliant idea." Amelia clapped her hands. "No parent will be able to resist bringing their family to Stampede when they hear about the carnival rides."

Gunner nudged Reid's elbow. "The fairgrounds burned to the ground five years ago."

"That's right," Amelia said. "We're using the motel parking lot and the adjacent acreage for the rodeo."

"Who's in charge of booking the carnival?" Logan was still scribbling in his notebook.

"I'd be happy to make a few calls," Sadie said.

"I suppose you got something in mind for me to do," Emmett grumbled.

Amelia smiled. "As mayor you'll have to sign the permits, then your job is to stay out of my way."

"Fine by me. I'll pack my things and move out of your house tonight."

"Emmett, if you'd like your room back, I'm more than happy to stay at the motel," Scarlett said.

Amelia scoffed. "Emmett's fine right where he is."

Reid swore his grandfather's mouth had curved into a smile before he bit into a piece of chicken.

"Speaking of my house—" Amelia pushed her chair back and stood "—we need to get home, Emmett. I told Gladys I'd return her call about the ladies' luncheon next week."

His grandfather's mouth dropped open. "We haven't had dessert."

"I'll wrap up a dish of peach cobbler for you to take home." Sadie left the room and Amelia followed, saying, "Not too much. Emmett has a huge bowl of ice cream every night before bed."

"I'm done, Dad," Tommy said. "Can I leave the table?"

Logan nodded, then looked at Tyler, who hadn't finished his peas. "Go ahead."

The boys pushed their chairs in, then raced out of the room.

"I'm impressed," Reid said. "We never put our chairs back after leaving the table."

Logan almost cracked a smile. "It takes about three months to teach the twins a new trick."

Scarlett gathered armfuls of dishes. "Let me help," Reid said.

"No, thanks." Scarlett looked at Jessie. "We've got this."

Jessie grabbed the bowl of mashed potatoes and ducked out of the room, leaving the men alone.

"Everything okay between you and Amelia?" Reid asked his grandfather. The woman acted like she was the mayor and not his grandfather.

"She's getting too big for her britches, but you ought to see how many gallons of ice cream fit into that fancy fridge she's got in her house." The old man headed for the exit. "I want to make sure Sadie gives me a big enough helping of cobbler."

Left alone with his brothers, Reid squirmed under their stares. "I heard you and Scarlett went out to look at the cabin this afternoon," Logan said. "Since the petting zoo opened and we've been giving trail rides, I've managed to build up a small savings if you want to make a few updates."

"I don't want you to waste your money," Reid said.

"It wouldn't be a waste of money if you plan to stay."

Was Logan suggesting that Reid and Jessie should live permanently on the ranch?

"We better say goodbye to the old folks," Gunner said. "And I need to get back over to the hospital."

Reid followed his brothers into the hallway, noting the new clock on the wall by the front door and another one on the table in the foyer. What was up with all the clocks?

They joined the rest of the family in the front yard. Amelia hugged the twins and even gave Jessie a hug. Sadie and Scarlett hugged the old couple. His grandfather hugged the twins and then he patted Jessie on the shoulder and said something that made her smile.

Reid watched the hug fest unfold, wondering what had happened to his family. The only person who'd hugged him growing up had been his grandmother.

Amelia and his grandfather got into the jalopy and drove off. The twins raced after the truck for several yards, then gave up the chase and walked back to the house.

"Gramps drives slow enough to let the boys think they can catch him," Logan said. "Sadie thought it was dangerous at first until I pointed out that the boys fall asleep faster at bedtime."

"I should remember that," Gunner said.

Reid doubted the idea would work with Jessie. He had a hunch girls would rather chase boys than cars.

"If you let kids think they're getting away with something once in a while, they don't test you as often," Logan said.

When the twins arrived at the porch, huffing and puffing, Sadie announced that it was bath time. Gunner waved goodbye and took off in his vehicle. Scarlett said she and Jessie would clean up the kitchen.

"Want to take a walk?" Logan asked.

"It's dark out."

His brother grabbed a camping flashlight from the table between the rockers. "I'll show you the tree house I built for the boys."

They cut through the yard, past their grandmother's garden. Reid noticed the white-picket fence was new. "How come you let Amelia coerce you and Gramps into turning the ranch into a tourist attraction?"

"I didn't have a choice."

"What do you mean?"

Logan continued walking, shining the light along the path. "I messed up the ranch finances and accidentally skipped a few mortgage payments."

Accidentally?

"The tree house is over there." He directed the light at a large river oak.

"We built a house in that same tree once," Reid said. "Only ours didn't look as nice."

"Gunner fell through the floor and broke his arm." Logan grinned. "Remember that?"

Reid chuckled. "Gramps had to drive him to hospital because mom got one of her a migraines."

"Then Grandma came out here, saw the tree house and made Gramps tear it down."

"But I was the one who got yelled at for leading you and Gunner astray. Gramps punished me with more chores and Gunner got his favorite cake for desert that night." Logan looked at Reid. "I don't remember what happened to you."

When Reid thought back to that afternoon, he hadn't recalled his brothers being there when their father had come home and blamed him for Gunner getting hurt. Reid remembered the incident as if it happened yesterday. He'd been riding his bike in the yard and his father had snuck up behind him and grabbed the back of his shirt, yanking him off the bike. Keeping hold of Reid's collar, his dad had dragged him behind the barn out of the view of the kitchen window. There he'd let loose a string of ugly words that inflicted more harm than a belt-whipping.

Reid shook off the memory. "Is the tree house sturdy enough to hold us?"

"Yep." Logan climbed the four steps nailed to the trunk, then Reid followed. They sat across from each other, their knees pulled up to their chests. Logan shut off the lantern and the glow of the full moon streamed through the branches above their heads.

"What happened to the money I've been sending home?" *For years.*

"I opened a savings account for Gramps and I've been depositing your checks in there."

"Why not put it toward the mortgage?"

"I wanted to make sure that if anything happened to Gramps we could afford to pay a visiting nurse to look after him." Logan drew in a deep breath. "After all he did for us through the years, he doesn't deserve to be put into a home."

"You could have told me you were in financial trouble. I would have loaned you money."

"Gunner suggested the same thing."

"Why didn't you call me?" Reid asked.

"I was angry."

"About what?"

"You walked out on our family and never came back. Just like Mom."

Reid stared at his clasped hands. He couldn't deny the charge—he'd done exactly what Logan had accused him of. Feeling cornered he went on the attack. "I doubt you noticed my absence."

"I sure in hell did when it was just me up at 5:00 a.m. feeding cattle and mucking stalls."

"Where was Gunner?"

"You know he never liked ranch chores." Logan snorted.

"That's because you and I picked up the slack."

When their father was home even Logan got out of a few chores but not Reid—his father doubled down on him.

"Why didn't you come home after you left the military?"

"I needed to decompress." That was partly true. Transitioning back into civilian life took a while.

"The first time I saw Gramps scared was when he told Gunner and me that you'd been sent to Afghanistan."

"I was fine." Reid had done two years at Camp Dwyer in the Garmsir District of the Helmand Province in southern Afghanistan.

"I had it easy as a mechanic." Only once had he risked his life accompanying his battalion on a reconnaissance mission to recover a Stryker tank that had been abandoned after it had engine trouble. Reid had been fortunate that he hadn't witnessed the horrors his comrades had.

"I told Gramps if anyone could survive over there, it was you," Logan said.

"How so?" Reid asked.

"You're quiet. You don't make waves." Logan shrugged. "I figured you were always thinking and analyzing your next move."

Reid was taken aback that his brother thought he'd been quiet because he was smart. He'd tried not draw attention to himself, because he hadn't wanted to give their father a reason to lash out at him.

"Maybe if I'd been more like you and stayed out of trouble, I would have had it easier growing up."

Logan thought he'd had a difficult childhood?

"Remember when I pegged you in the back of the

head with an apple after we got off the school bus?"
Logan said.

His brother had saved the apple from his lunch and
had thought it would be funny to throw it at Reid's head.
"I didn't know you could move that fast."

"I'm surprised I didn't break an ankle running back
and forth, trying to dodge the rocks you aimed at me,"
Logan said. "You had a hell of an arm even before you
played baseball in high school."

"I could have hit you, if I'd wanted to. I would have
chased you into the house but Gunner tripped me and
I fell down. The next thing I heard was mom screaming." Their mother had been standing at the stove fry-
ing bacon when Logan had raced into the kitchen and
plowed into her. Hot grease had spilled on her arm,
causing second-degree burns from her wrist to her
elbow.

"Sometimes when I close my eyes, I can still hear
Mom's cries." Logan leaned his head against the trunk.
"I was always screwing up."

His brother would get no argument from Reid on
that point. When Logan had been assigned a chore he'd
forget or quit halfway through and run off to do something else. And every time Logan bailed, Reid would
have to finish his tasks. "You never followed through
on anything."

"There's a reason I didn't."

Reid wanted to laugh but Logan's sober expression
stopped him.

"Last year I was diagnosed with attention deficit
disorder."

"Are you serious?"

"When the bank threatened to foreclose on the property, Amelia asked Sadie to go over the ranch books, because I swore I had kept up with the mortgage payments."

"What did she find?"

"I'd skipped three payments and hadn't even opened the late notices from the bank."

Reid whistled between his teeth.

"The doctor put me on meds but I hated the way the pills made me feel so I quit taking them. I thought I could manage my inability to focus, but things got busy at the ranch when the septic system went out and a storm knocked down a bunch of trees on the property, and then the engine in Gramps' truck died."

"Where was Gunner when all that was happening?"

"Rodeoing or chasing women." Logan shoved a hand through his hair. "I considered asking you to come home and help, but I figured you couldn't leave your job."

His brother was being nice by blaming Reid's job when they both knew he would have said no regardless. "I'm sorry." The apology sounded inadequate, especially now that he knew his brother's behavior growing up hadn't been intentional. He wondered if their father had guessed Logan's problem.

"The ranch is busier now that you have a petting zoo and give trail rides," Reid said. "How are you handling it all by yourself?"

"Things changed when Sadie and the boys showed up last summer. Tommy has ADD, too."

"I noticed he has trouble sitting still."

"Tyler reminds me of you," Logan said. "He's quiet, smart and thoughtful."

Thoughtful? Had his brother really not known that all the times Reid had picked up the slack for him, he hadn't done so out of the goodness of his heart, but because their father had threatened Reid with punishment if he didn't?

"Until I saw how Tommy's behavior took attention away from Tyler, I didn't realize that I'd probably done the same thing to you and Gunner."

The longer they discussed the past the more confused Reid grew. He'd left home because he'd never felt like he belonged in their family. He'd convinced himself that his brothers had had it easy growing up, but obviously Logan had been dealing with his own issues and had walked away from their childhood with baggage, too.

"I remember the time Dad came home and said he was having trouble with the engine in his truck and you fixed it for him."

Reid had been sixteen that summer. He'd heard his dad complain to Gramps that he needed a new pickup but Gramps wouldn't loan him the money.

That evening Reid had snuck out of the house after everyone was sleeping and he'd parked the truck inside the barn and had worked on the engine all night. By sunrise he'd had it purring like a kitten. He'd parked the pickup in the yard and had gone to bed with a smile on his face, believing that for once his old man would be forced to acknowledge Reid's good deed.

By the time he woke up a few hours later, his father and the pickup were gone. When Reid asked if his dad had said anything about the engine working, Gramps shook his head and walked off. It was then that Reid knew nothing he ever did would be good enough.

"How are you managing your ADD now?" Reid asked.

"I see a behavioral therapist once a month and he teaches me coping strategies."

"Is that why there are so many clocks in the house?"

"You noticed." Logan raised his arm. "I wear a watch now. And I write myself notes. Each night Sadie and I go over the next day's plans. Anytime someone asks me to do something that's not on my list, I tell them to call Sadie."

"Is Sadie the ranch operation's manager then?"

Logan nodded. "She used to keep the books for a dental office in Madison but got laid off from her job before she and the boys came down to visit Amelia."

"What's up with the twins' father?"

"He lives in Ohio with his girlfriend and her kids."

A shrill whistle echoed through the woods and Logan scrambled to his feet. "That's Sadie. The boys are ready for bed."

Reid climbed out of the tree surprised that he was disappointed their conversation had ended abruptly.

They returned to the yard but before they reached the back porch, Logan stopped. "None of us can change the past and I won't hold it against you if you decide to leave again, but for what's it worth…this is still your home." Logan went into the house.

Reid was glad he and his brother had talked, even if it left him with more questions than answers. Logan's words had been heartfelt but Paradise Ranch still didn't feel like home. Reid sat on the steps and listened to the unfamiliar sounds of bleating goats, and pig grunts.

The back door opened and Jessie and Fang joined him. She lifted the hem of her sweatshirt and the dog burrowed under the cover.

"Are you sleeping at the motel tonight?" she asked.

"I'd planned to. If you want to stay here, I can drive into town and get your things for you."

"Okay, sure."

She hadn't even hesitated. "Jessie," he said, "are you uncomfortable around me?"

"Sometimes."

"If you've don't want to live with me—"

Her head snapped toward him. "I thought you wanted us to be together."

He was going about this wrong. "That's not it," he said. "I just assumed you had a change of heart."

"Why would you think that?" Her voice rose in pitch.

He hadn't meant to upset her. "Because you still haven't called me Dad."

"That's because you don't feel like a dad yet."

Her words stabbed him in the chest. He felt physically ill at the thought of Jessie harboring the same feelings toward him that he'd held for his father. He changed the subject. "Tell me about your mother."

"You don't remember her?"

"I remember Stacy, but we were eighteen when we…"

"I'm twelve. I know how babies are made."

Reid's cheeks grew warm and he was glad it was dark outside. With the amount of time Jessie spent on the internet doing her studies, he was sure she knew a whole lot more than where babies came from.

Scarlett stepped outside. "Jessie, Sadie wants to know if you plan to sleep here tonight. She'll make up the couch in the office, if you are."

"She is." Reid stood. "I'll head over to the motel and get her things now."

The man had not only broken her heart but he'd almost ruined her career.

"I never pictured our baby brother as a father." Logan patted Gunner's back.

"You and me both." Gunner pulled Lydia close. "And I never thought I'd find a woman who makes me this happy." He kissed his wife and the twins stuck their fingers in their mouths and made gagging noises.

"Kissing's gross," Tommy said. "Right, Tyler?" His brother nodded.

"Is that so?" Logan caught Sadie's hand and tugged her against him. "Can I get gross with you, Mrs. Hardell?"

"Please do, Mr. Hardell." Sadie and Logan kissed.

Tommy slapped his hands over his eyes. "Yuck!"

The adults laughed and then Tommy tugged on Emmett's pants. "Gramps, you're not gonna kiss Aunt Amelia, are you?"

Amelia's cheeks glowed red. "For goodness sake, boys, stop pestering the adults."

"I want some cake!" Tommy batted a balloon tied to a chair and it bounced off the back of Emmett's head.

"Okay, guys," Logan said. "Come with me until Mom's ready to serve the cake." Logan took the twins by their hands and escorted them from the room.

"We'll make a pot of coffee," Emmett said, following Amelia out the door.

"I'll fetch the paper plates and forks." Sadie trailed after the old folks into the kitchen.

Scarlett was left alone with Lydia, Gunner, Reid and Jessie. Reid smiled at the new mother. "It's nice to meet you, Lydia. Congratulations on the baby."

"Thank you," she said. "I'm glad you could be here for our special occasion."

Reid waved Jessie over. "My daughter, Jessie."

"Hi, Jessie," Lydia said. "Welcome to Stampede."

Jessie peered at the baby. "She's really small."

"Seven pounds twelve ounces," Gunner said.

"Have you been around many babies?" Lydia asked Jessie.

She shook her head. "Nope."

"Would you like to hold her?" Lydia asked.

Gunner stared at his wife as if she'd lost her mind. The overprotective daddy gene had already kicked in.

"No, thanks." Jessie backed up a step and then made a hasty exit.

"She has your eyes, Reid," Lydia said.

Scarlett smiled. "The exact same shade of blue."

Lydia transferred the baby into Gunner's arms and the look of love on his face was heartwarming. When Scarlett glanced at Reid, she was taken aback by the sadness in his eyes.

"Excuse me." Reid left the room and a moment later the front door opened and closed.

"Do you need help with little Amelia?" Scarlett asked.

Lydia's eyes went to the doorway. "We're fine."

Scarlett found Reid sitting on the porch swing, his gaze fixated on the gravel road. "Mind if I join you?" She didn't wait for an invitation and sat down next to him. Then she closed her eyes and breathed in the sandalwood scent of Reid's cologne. "What's on your mind?"

He dragged his gaze from the driveway. "Thinking about tomorrow."

"Another manic Monday."

"What time do you go into work?" he asked.

"Seven thirty. My boss asked me to come in early to talk about a new client she's assigning to me. Then I have three home visits scheduled and I'll be tied up at the office late doing paperwork."

"Sounds hectic."

"It will be but then there are other days when clients cancel and I'm able to leave work early." She nudged his arm. "What are you doing tomorrow?"

"Calling rodeo stock contractors for Amelia. After that I'll do a few minor repairs to the cabin. Maybe Jessie and I will drive into Mesquite and check out the resale shop you suggested."

"It's on Main Street. You can't miss it." Their gazes connected for a moment before his eyes drifted to her mouth. If only they had more privacy, she'd initiate their second kiss.

"What else is bothering you?" she asked, then added, "Sorry, poking my nose into other people's lives is a bad habit I've gotten good at because of my job."

"I'm jealous of my brothers," he said.

"Why?"

"The twins aren't even Logan's biological kids, but you'd never know that by the way he treats them. And Gunner…" Reid leaned forward and clasped his hands between his knees. "The look on his face when he stared at the baby…" Reid expelled a sharp breath. "In my head I've accepted that I'm Jessie's father, but in my heart all I feel is anxiety and fear."

Scarlett's profession had taught her that some parents never bonded with their child no matter how hard they tried or how much they yearned to. Those situations rarely ended well for anyone in the family. "Do you view Jessie as a responsibility?"

"Of course I do, and I'd never walk away from her."

He sounded like a marine speaking, not a father. "There are lots of ways to be responsible for Jessie and take care of her without being involved in her day-to-day life."

"I want a lasting relationship with Jessie, Scarlett. I just don't know how to make it happen."

"You can't rush these things. The more you do together the faster she'll drop her guard."

Silence stretched between them, then he said, "You and your cousins seem close."

"We grew up in Madison together. Even though we went to different high schools we socialized on the weekends and shared the same group of friends. After college we all found jobs in the city. When Sadie had the twins, Lydia and I took turns watching the boys and attending their sporting events and activities." She bumped shoulders with him. "And then my cousins fell in love with your brothers and ruined everything."

"What do you mean?"

"They moved away and left me all alone in Wisconsin. Whenever I spoke with Sadie or Lydia all they'd brag about is how much they loved living in Stampede and how happy they were." Scarlett remembered how low she'd felt after their conversations. She'd been lonely and vulnerable when Dale had come along and taken advantage of her.

"Did your cousins talk you into moving here or did you come on your own?"

Scarlett hadn't told Sadie and Lydia the real reason she'd packed her things and moved south. She was too mortified to tell them the whole truth. "After Dale and I broke up I needed a change of scenery. A fresh start."

He smiled.

"What?"

"Is dating again part of your fresh start?"

She laughed. "Are you applying for the job?"

"Maybe."

"I love your enthusiasm."

"It's been a while since I've mingled with the opposite sex." His gaze swept across the yard. "After I found out about Jessie, I put that part of my life on hold." He leaned back and crossed his arms over his chest. "I never intended to marry because I never wanted kids."

"Did you have a backup plan in case you ended up having a kid?"

He chuckled. "No. I'm winging it, which probably isn't smart after my dysfunctional upbringing."

"What do you mean?"

He swept his arm out in front of him. "The house and barn have a fresh coat of paint, the driveway's been repaired, my grandmother's garden has been restored. It's as if the run-down homestead with a cheating father, a dying grandmother and a mom who abandoned her kids had never existed."

"I don't think anyone in your family has forgotten the past. I think they've chosen to move on."

"Obviously, because Gunner and Logan make fatherhood look easy."

Scarlett understood Reid's jealousy. She'd been envious of her cousins when they'd found happiness and she'd found heartache.

"Don't tell anyone I said this but your brothers aren't

perfect," she whispered. "Gunner was a wreck the entire time Lydia was pregnant. You would have thought he was the one carrying their baby. And Sadie says Logan is too easy on the twins even after she's had numerous talks with him about discipline."

"Thanks—" he grinned "—but that doesn't make me feel better."

"I can't speak from personal experience," she said, "but what I've witnessed in my career is that parenting is something you learn as you go. You'll make mistakes but then you'll have successes, too. In the end they usually balance each other out."

"If I want permanent custody of Jessie, I don't have room to make mistakes."

"Give her a little space and respect her boundaries and she'll open up."

His breath fanned Scarlett's cheek. "What about your boundaries? Do I have to respect those, too?"

If she turned her head, his mouth would almost touch hers—so she did. "That depends."

"On what?"

"On which boundary you want to overstep."

"Kissing?"

Anticipation hummed through her body. "Kissing is permissible."

Reid's hand settled on her thigh right before his mouth nuzzled her ear.

"Where's my dad?" Jessie's voice echoed inside the house.

Reid bolted from the swing and retreated to the opposite end of the porch.

Scarlett smiled. "You're not going to fool anyone by standing over there."

"I'm not?"

Her gaze dropped to his crotch.

He cursed, then whipped off his cowboy hat and placed it in front of him, pretending to examine the brim, as his daughter stepped onto the porch.

"I thought you'd left." Jessie glanced between the adults.

"We were enjoying the nice weather," Reid said.

Oh, brother. "Actually we were gossiping about family." Scarlett winked at Jessie. "Where's Fang?"

"The boys are taking turns holding him."

"Did you need something?" Reid asked.

"Aunt Sadie wants to know if you guys are having cake."

"Yes." Scarlett went to the door, then looked over her shoulder. "Are you coming?"

"I'll be there in a minute."

Scarlett flashed an impish smile, enjoying his discomfort. It had been a long time since she'd had that kind of effect on a man, and she couldn't wait to see if there was more in their future than just mutual attraction.

REID LOOKED HIMSELF over in the motel-room mirror Tuesday morning. He was meeting a stock contractor at his ranch north of Laredo to discuss supplying the Stampede rodeo with broncs and bulls. Wanting to make a good impression Reid had dressed up for the occasion—Western shirt, fresh-pressed jeans, a belt with a big buckle and his cowboy hat.

He checked the time on his cell phone. Gunner had offered to ride along with him today and Reid agreed to swing by his apartment at eight o'clock to pick him up.

He grabbed his wallet off the nightstand, then headed out to his pickup. When he reached the end of Chuck Wagon Drive, he took his foot off the gas and turned into the lot behind the building where Gunner and Lydia lived. He pulled alongside his brother's truck and then did a double take when he saw Gunner snoozing in the front seat. His brother had left the front window down so Reid walked over and stuck his hand inside the cab, then tapped the horn.

Gunner jerked upright. "What happened?"

"Did you sleep out here all night?"

His brother wiped the drool off his chin. "The baby's colicky and I walked the floors with her until 5:00 a.m. before Lydia took over. Then I couldn't fall asleep to all the crying, so I came out here to grab a nap."

"Tell you what." Reid braced his hands on the door frame. "Go back to bed. I'll meet with the contractor on my own."

"You sure?"

Reid nodded. "I'll let you know how it goes."

"Will you stop by the motel on your way out of town and tell Virginia that I'll be in at noon to relieve her?"

"Sure."

"Appreciate it." Gunner stumbled up the fire escape and entered the apartment.

Reid returned to the Moonlight. The smell of coffee greeted him when he entered the office. "Mornin'," he said.

A short woman with spiked auburn hair and bright pink lipstick smiled. "You must be Reid Hardell." She stepped from behind the counter wearing a pair of tight leggings and a top a size too small for her ample bosom.

"Virginia Phillips. I live across the street from Amelia Rinehart."

"Nice to meet you," he said.

"I moved here with my husband twenty years ago and I remember your brothers but not you."

He wasn't surprised.

"Logan was good at rodeo and Gunner was good at getting into trouble." She laughed. "Folks still talk about the giant ta-tas Gunner spray-painted on the back of the Woolworth building." Her gaze ran over Reid. "Gosh darn, I think you're the best-looking brother out of the bunch. Those blue eyes are giving me heart palpitations."

Reid was used to women staring at him but not ladies old enough to be his mother.

"Can I make you a cup of coffee?" she asked.

"No, thanks. I stopped in to give you a message from Gunner."

"What's that?"

"The baby kept him up all night and he won't be going out of town today. He'll be in at noon to take over for you."

She patted her teased hair. "Well, then, I think I'll make an appointment at the beauty salon and touch up my color."

"It was nice meeting you, Virginia."

"Likewise. And welcome home."

Reid hopped into his truck and started the engine, then inputted the stock contractor's address into the GPS system. Before he'd finished, a horn honked. He checked the side mirror and spotted Scarlett's white Camry pulling up to the motel. He watched her stroll over to his truck, taking in her outfit—jeans, cowgirl boots and a yellow plaid shirt. She sure didn't dress like Jessie's former social worker in El Paso. Maybe she had the day off.

He lowered the passenger-side window and smiled. "You look like a Texas cowgirl, not a dairy maiden."

She didn't return his smile. "Where's Jessie?"

"Logan offered to take her out to the riding stable and show her the trail horses. I'm driving to Laredo to meet with a stock contractor." Something was off about Scarlett, but her eyes were hidden behind a pair of sunglasses. "What's up?"

"We need to talk." The serious note in her voice surprised him.

"What's the matter? Did Fang cause trouble last night at the house?"

"Nothing like that." She looked at his GPS screen. "Are you coming right back after your meeting?"

"I am."

"Do you mind if tag along?"

He wondered why she asked, because she sure didn't sound like she wanted to go for a drive with him. "Aren't you working today?"

"This is work." She removed the shades—there wasn't an ounce of warmth in her brown eyes. "Let me lock up my car and I'll explain everything."

Explain what? He waited for Scarlett to climb into the cab and buckle up. Maybe food would put her in a better mood. "Have you had breakfast?"

"No."

He shifted into Reverse and backed out of the parking spot, then headed into town for the second time that morning. He parked on the street in front of the Cattle Drive Café. "Bagels and coffee okay?"

Her phone went off. "Yes, thanks. I have to take this call."

He left her in the truck and entered the café. A middle-aged waitress waved him over to the lunch counter. "What can I get you, handsome?"

"Bagels if you have any."

"Bagels?" Dark eyebrows inched up the woman's forehead. "Does this place look like an uppity city eatery? The closest thing we got to a bagel is raisin toast or powdered doughnuts." She squinted at him. "You're not from here, are you?"

"I grew up in Stampede, ma'am."

She slapped her hand over her chest and gasped. The patrons sitting at the counter looked their way. "Reid Hardell."

"Yes, ma'am."

"Well, I'll be." She smiled. "You Hardell brothers sure are a handsome bunch."

"I'll take two slices of raisin toast and a half dozen doughnuts. Two black coffees and two bottles of water."

"To go?"

"Yes, ma'am."

Five minutes later she set a paper sack on the counter. "Name's Dolly by the way."

He pulled out a twenty and dropped the bill on the counter. "I appreciate the service."

Dolly blushed. "You tell Gunner we all want to see little Amelia when Lydia feels up to bringing the baby in."

"Will do."

"The same goes for you," Dolly said.

"Pardon?"

"Bring your daughter in so we can meet her."

Reid glanced at the customers nearby and several heads bobbed. He'd been gone so long that he'd forgotten people had nothing better to do in small towns than poke their noses into other people's business. "Yes, ma'am."

Reid tipped his hat and returned to his pickup. He handed Scarlett the tray holder with the coffees, then got behind the wheel. "They don't sell bagels," he said. "Breakfast is raisin toast and doughnuts." He transferred his coffee to a cup holder before starting the engine.

She opened the bag. "What would you like?"

"A doughnut." He needed the sugar to calm the jittery feeling he got from her aloofness. He ate the pastry as he drove out of town, then took a sip of coffee before entering the on-ramp to the highway.

"Are you nervous about your meeting with the contractor?" she asked.

"No." But *she* was making him nervous. "Should I be?"

"If things don't go well, Aunt Amelia will be disappointed. And if she's disappointed, she'll give your grandfather an earful. And if your grandfather gets an earful from her—"

"He'll walk about like a bear with a bee stinger stuck in his lip."

"Exactly."

What was up with all the small talk? He flipped on the blinker and merged with traffic. "So to what do I owe the pleasure of your company this morning?"

She drew in a deep breath, then blew it out slowly.

"Shoot, Scarlett," he said. "Just spit it out."

"I've been assigned to Jessie's case."

"What are you talking about?"

"I'm her new social worker."

Chapter Six

"What do you mean you're Jessie's new caseworker?" Reid looked confused—almost as perplexed as Scarlett had been when her boss had broken the news to her.

"Mrs. Delgado reached out to my manager last week and arranged to transfer Jessie's case to the office in Mesquite."

"I get that El Paso is too far away for Mrs. Delgado to keep tabs on the situation, but why would they assign you to Jessie's case when we're practically family?"

"Normally they wouldn't," she said, "but rural social workers are in short supply and one of the employees in our office just went out on medical leave and my boss made an exception." Scarlett had challenged Lois, offering to switch clients with another coworker, but her boss wouldn't budge and Scarlett felt as if she couldn't refuse without having to reveal the story behind her resignation from the job in Madison.

She hated to put the brakes on her and Reid's relationship before it had even gotten off the ground, but her confidence in her ability to do her job needed a boost and this was an opportunity to prove to herself that her mistake with Dale had been a fluke, and she still possessed good judgment.

"What does that mean for us?" he asked.

"It means we can't…" Good grief, it wasn't as if they'd already crawled into bed with each other. "We have to maintain a professional relationship."

His mouth twitched. "It's a little late for that, don't you think?" Then he frowned. "You're joking, right?"

"I'm afraid not." She hated having to reveal her naïveté, but Reid needed to understand the seriousness of their situation. "I made the mistake of falling for the father of one of my clients."

Reid glanced her way. "Was that the guy you were engaged to?"

She nodded. Dale had made a fool out of her in front of her colleagues and had damaged her confidence in her ability to judge people. "He was a single father, trying to gain full custody of his daughter."

"I'm listening."

"I'd been working with Amy for about two years. Her parents were divorced and her father was employed overseas." She waved her hand. "It was a complicated mess. Anyway, Dale moved back to the states after Amy's mother went into drug rehab for the third time." She glanced at Reid but his gaze remained on the road.

"Dale found a job in Madison but because he'd been absent from Amy's life for long periods of time, she'd been placed in a foster home and I chaperoned visits between them." She'd gone on picnics in the park with the pair and Dale had scheduled a bowling and pizza night once a week. Amy's father was handsome and charming and when he began whispering in her ear that he was falling in love with her, Scarlett had gotten caught up in the fantasy of being a family.

Reid touched the back of her hand and the memories

evaporated. "Sorry," she mumbled. "Dale was a good father and I recommended that he get full custody of Amy, but the court date for the hearing was scheduled for nine months out." She drew in a deep breath. "Then he took me by surprise a few weeks later and asked me to marry him. The following week we went house hunting with a Realtor." It had all been a scheme to convince her that he wanted to build a life with her. "Because we were engaged I was able to pull a few strings and move the court date up by several months and Dale was awarded permanent custody of Amy."

"Then what happened?" Reid asked.

"Two days went by after the hearing and Dale wasn't returning my calls. I got worried and went over to his apartment." Even now her eyes still stung remembering when she'd demanded the manager let her into the apartment so she could see for herself that Dale had moved out. "The place was empty. I called Amy's school and the principal said Dale had withdrawn her the day before."

"Where did he go?"

She shrugged. "He told the principal he'd gotten a new job in California but I'm sure he lied about that, too." For all she knew he'd gone back overseas with his daughter.

"I'm sorry, Scarlett."

"There's more." She'd tell him every humiliating detail, so he'd understand why they couldn't cross the line with each other. "The engagement ring Dale bought me was a cubic zirconia." The schmuck had shattered her heart and almost ruined her life, but she still remembered how excited she'd been when he'd slid that ring over her finger. She'd thought she'd finally have what her cousins had found with their husbands.

"He played me until he was sure he'd win full custody of Amy, then he took off." She'd gotten over Dale but it had taken longer for her bruised heart to let go of Amy. His daughter had genuinely cared about Scarlett, and she'd loved the little girl as if she was her biological mother. "I'm sure Dale put all the blame on me for the breakup and Amy probably despises me."

"I'm not using you, Scarlett. I don't need you to help me gain custody of Jessie."

"I know that, but—"

"I'll demand a different social worker."

"No, don't," she said. "That'll raise red flags with my supervisor and I've only been on the job a few months."

He was silent for a long time, then he asked, "What if we don't tell anyone we're seeing each other?"

"It's too risky. We can be friends, but that's pushing it."

"Friends who kiss?"

He looked so hopeful. "No kissing."

"How long will the whole process of gaining permanent custody of Jessie take?"

"Once I'm convinced you two are comfortable with each other and Jessie wants to be with you, then I petition the courts on your behalf and we receive a date to appear before the judge."

He looked at Scarlett with a determined glint in his eye. "I'll work hard then to prove that Jessie belongs with me."

Under any other circumstance Scarlett would be flattered that a man wanted to be with her so badly, but she worried Reid was focusing on the wrong goal.

Instead of discussing an action plan for Jessie, they made the rest of the hour-and-a-half drive in virtual silence. When they arrived at the ranch Colonel Finley whisked Reid off to look at the bulls and broncs and Scarlett stayed behind to check work emails. After answering several inquiries she put her phone away and got out of the pickup. The front door opened and a statuesque woman walked out of the house.

The long-legged lady approached Scarlett and offered her hand. "I'm Reyna. The colonel's granddaughter."

"Scarlett Johnson."

"I was surprised when my grandfather said Stampede was bringing their rodeo back."

"You're familiar with the town?"

The brunette smiled. "I'd never heard of Stampede until I ran into Logan and Gunner on the circuit." Her brow scrunched. "I don't recall meeting the middle brother Reid."

The beautiful woman could have her pick of men but her ring finger was bare. "My cousin Lydia married Gunner. They just had a baby girl a few days ago."

"Gunner's a father?" Reyna smiled. "I can't picture that cowboy settling down." Her gaze shifted to the pasture beyond the corrals. "I heard Logan married and left the circuit to help his grandfather run Paradise Ranch."

"He and his first wife divorced. He's now married to my other cousin and they have twin sons."

"And Reid?" Her gaze drifted over Scarlett. "Is he still available?"

Jealousy pricked Scarlett. On Sunday she would have told the woman to take a hike, but she didn't dare say anything that would hint at a personal relationship between her and Reid. She couldn't risk her boss receiving an anonymous tip about inappropriate behavior with the father of one of her clients. "Reid's a single father. He just moved back to Stampede."

"Father?"

"He has a twelve-year-old daughter."

Reyna's gaze swung to the pasture again where the colonel and Reid stood with their boots propped on the bottom fence rail. "You said *single* father?"

"Yes." The word escaped through clenched teeth.

Hoping to distract Reyna, Scarlett said, "My great-aunt Amelia Rinehart is behind the plans to revive the Stampede Rodeo and Spring Festival."

"Good for her. I admire strong women." Reyna pulled her gaze away from the men. "Are you here because you're helping with the rodeo?"

"Actually I'm a social worker and Reid's daughter is my client."

"That's great." Reyna smiled.

Yeah, just great. "It looks like they're coming back."

The colonel parked the pickup in the driveway and the men joined the ladies. "Reyna Finley." She extended a hand to Reid. "I compete in barrel racing on the circuit and ran into your brothers from time to time."

"Reid Hardell," he said.

"Your daughter's social worker—" Reyna nodded to Scarlett "—said you're back in Stampede now."

Reid nodded, then pulled out his wallet and removed a business card. Reyna lifted her hand, expecting Reid to offer her the card, but instead he gave it to her grandfather. "Logan's wife, Sadie, handles all the paperwork."

"I'll email a contract to her later today," the colonel said.

The men shook hands, then the colonel spoke to his granddaughter. "I need your advice on a bull I've had my eye on." He took her by the arm and they walked off, Reyna looking over her shoulder at Reid. "Call me if there's anything I can do to help with the rodeo." She smiled, then turned away, hips waving like a racing flag as she followed her grandfather to his pickup.

"Ready?" Reid approached the passenger-side door and Scarlett cut him off, grabbing the handle first. "I forgot," he muttered, then walked around the hood and got behind the wheel and started the engine. "I guess holding a door open for you is off-limits now?"

"Especially in front of a woman who wants to crawl into bed with you."

He grinned. "You noticed that, too, huh?" He drove toward the highway. "Do you mind if we stop at the Walmart on the way back to Stampede?"

"That's fine."

"I'd like to buy a pet carrier for Fang. Sadie's been nice enough to let Jessie keep him in the house, but I overheard her tell Logan that the dog gets in the way when she's cooking."

"Is the colonel the only stock contractor Gunner recommended?" she asked.

"He gave me more names."

"And you didn't want to check with the other contractors before making a final decision?"

"The colonel's a fair man. I won't get a better deal from anyone else."

"How do you know he's fair?" she asked.

"The colonel served in the Army. Whether he's fighting for our country or running a business, his core values don't change." Reid looked at her. "He'll honor the price he quoted and deliver his best stock and more important, the animals will be in good shape and well cared for before, during and after the rodeo."

"In my job you can't trust anyone."

"What do you mean?"

"With family relationships it's difficult to know who's lying and who's telling the truth. I have to go with my gut." And, boy, had Scarlett's gut gotten it wrong with Dale. "Sometimes parents and guardians say and do what's in their best interest and not the child's. You learn pretty quickly not to take people at their word."

"There are always two sides to every story," he said.

"In my experience people often pick the wrong side and the children pay the price."

"Why did you get into social work, if it's such a challenge?"

"Someone has to protect those who can't protect themselves."

"I admire you advocating for kids. I'm sure it's not easy seeing what happens to some of them." He glanced at Scarlett and her heart beat a little faster at the warm compassion in his eyes.

She pretended interest in the scenery outside her window. "What was your time like in the military?"

"Are you asking as Jessie's social worker?"

"Yes." And no.

"After I made it through boot camp, I received additional mechanics training on large engines. I spent most of my time in Afghanistan working on combat vehicles and tanks."

"Did anything bad happen over there?"

"To me personally, you mean?"

She nodded.

"If you're concerned I have PTSD and might lash out at Jessie, I don't."

Scarlett winced at the anxiety in his eyes and wished she could calm his fears. "Reid, I don't like this any more than you do, but part of the process of determining if Jessie stays with you is finding out if there's anything in your background that might negatively affect her."

Scarlett changed the subject. "Do you still plan to ride in the rodeo?"

"That depends," he said.

"On what?"

His jaw clenched. "On whether you believe it helps or doesn't help my petition for custody."

This wasn't what she wanted—for Reid to feel defensive with her or that he had to seek her approval for everything he did. "It's not going to hurt your cause."

"Can I count on you to stop me from doing something that might jeopardize my case?"

"I have to treat you as I would any other client, Reid, but I'll do everything I can without overstepping my bounds to help you and Jessie succeed. What's best for Jessie will always be my number-one priority. Your daughter's welfare comes first."

"Understood."

She doubted he understood, but he'd accepted the situation.

"The Walmart is up ahead."

"I'll wait in the truck," she said, after he parked in the lot. They could both use a few minutes alone to digest their new relationship.

Reid's phone beeped with a text message. "It's Jessie," he said. "She wants to know when I'll be home."

He texted her back, then slipped the phone into his pocket. "I'll leave the keys in the ignition."

"Okay." Scarlett watched him walk off, proud of herself for not making any promises. She had to play this one by the book, which meant she'd have to stop talking about Reid with her cousins. Sadie had already mentioned that Reid had spent Monday working on the cabin, while Jessie played with the twins at the main house all day. Scarlett wondered what had happened to his plans to take Jessie shopping for furniture in Mesquite. And she also wondered if Reid realized he should be supervising Jessie's schoolwork or looking for someone who could. The twins might be on spring break, but his daughter wasn't.

"WHAT'S GOING ON?" Jessie asked when Reid and Scarlett returned to the ranch. He'd texted her to meet him outside to see the surprise he'd bought for her.

He tossed a bag of red licorice at her.

"Thanks." Jessie opened the package and pulled out a piece.

"That's not the surprise." Reid removed the blue pet carrier from the back seat. "I got this for Fang." He expected a smile or a thank-you—not the horrified look Jessie sent him.

"You want me to keep Fang in a cage all the time?"

"It's not a cage," he said. "Pets like to have their own space and since we don't have a doghouse for Fang, I thought this was the next best thing." He felt Scarlett's eyes on him and knew she was wondering why he didn't tell Jessie the truth—that the dog was wearing out its welcome in the house.

"No, thanks. Fang doesn't want it." Jessie went back inside.

Great. His first gesture of goodwill had failed and Scarlett had witnessed his defeat. He put the carrier back in the pickup. "I'll be at the cabin."

"Are you eating supper with the family?" she asked.

"No." He stared at her over the roof of the pickup. "Unless it's going to be held against me."

Scarlett folded her arms in front of her, the action pushing her breasts higher, reminding him in a painful way that he couldn't do a darn thing about his attraction to her. Before he got himself into more trouble, he drove off, clenching the steering wheel, his jaw and his toes inside his boots.

He was in over his head with this fatherhood stuff yet his brothers made it look so easy. Granted, little Amelia was a baby and the demands on Gunner consisted of feedings, changing diapers and snuggling. And the twins, who weren't Logan's biological sons, clamored to be with him.

But Reid never got it right with Jessie. Her reaction to the pet carrier reminded him of his father, who'd always looked at Reid with suspicious eyes.

He slowed down and turned onto the road that led to the back of the property, then parked in front of the cabin. He got out of the truck and stared at the front porch. Paint cans, supplies and tools sat on the steps. Leaning against the wall was a queen-size mattress and farther down the porch a single mattress and two sets of bedrails. In between the mattresses was a collection of large cardboard boxes with images of furniture printed on them. He took a closer look—a pub table and four chairs. Two end tables. A bookcase and a small desk, which he assumed was for Jessie. And wrapped in plastic was a love seat and matching chair.

He read the note taped to the front door. "Courtesy of Amelia Rinehart in payment for your work on the rodeo. Logan."

The matriarch of Stampede had more money than she knew what to do with. Years ago after she'd become a widow, Gramps had suggested she take her husband's millions and retire in the Bahamas. She'd ignored the advice and had stayed in Stampede. Reid suspected Amelia's reasons for not leaving town had more to do with his grandfather than her devotion to Stampede.

He spent the next half hour hauling the boxes and furniture inside, then he turned on the radio he'd found with the paint supplies and tuned it to a country station. Before he began putting the tables together he had a few general repairs to make. First on the list was adjusting the bedroom doors so they closed properly.

Willie Nelson's voice echoed through the cabin as Reid tightened the hinges and oiled the squeaky hardware. Next, he worked on the front door, installing a brand-new dead bolt he found in the supplies. A few minutes after he closed the door he heard a knock. Jessie stood on the porch carrying a cooler in one hand and Fang in the other. Her gaze skipped past him. "What's all that stuff?"

He moved aside and she entered the cabin. "Amelia bought us some furniture."

"Why?"

"For my help with the rodeo." He pointed to the cooler. "What did you bring?"

"Your supper."

"How did you get here?"

"Grandpa dropped me off."

"Grandpa? I thought you were calling him Emmett?"

"He threatened to make hot dogs out of Fang if I didn't call him grandpa." Jessie rolled her eyes. "I told him Fang is a Chihuahua, not a wiener dog, but he doesn't believe me."

"Go ahead and set Fang down. There's nothing he can get into."

She put the cooler on the counter, then removed Fang's leash. The dog dashed between the boxes, his little sniffer working overtime.

"I was about to fix a squeaky floorboard." Reid went into the bedroom and Jessie followed, hovering in the doorway.

"When are we moving in?" she asked.

"As soon as I get the beds and furniture put together."

"Your brothers don't think we're gonna stay," she said.

"How long we live here is up to you."

"Me?"

He nodded. "If you decide you don't like the ranch, then we'll go someplace else."

"Don't you want to be with your family?"

Reid didn't know how to answer that question, so he didn't.

"Are you going to eat the sandwich Scarlett made for you?"

Scarlett had packed his supper? He was surprised after she'd lectured him today about maintaining a professional relationship. Maybe she was having as tough a time reining in her attraction to him as he was his to her.

"There. That's done," he said, hammering the final

board. They returned to the main room. "What's everybody up to tonight?"

"Scarlett went over to Aunt Lydia's to see the baby." She handed him a ham sandwich and a can of soda, then grabbed a second can for herself.

Reid sat on the floor with his back against the front door and Fang sat next to him, tapping his paw against Reid's leg until he got a nibble of lunch meat.

"Which bedroom is mine?" Jessie asked.

"Take your pick. I don't care what room I sleep in." He finished the sandwich and took a swig of soda.

"Scarlett told me that she's my new case manager. She said we live too far away for Mrs. Delgado to check on me."

"How do you feel about that?"

Jessie shrugged. "It's weird since she's kind of like an aunt."

"Did you tell her that?"

"Scarlett said it wasn't her idea, but they don't have anyone else to help."

"We need to talk about your schooling." He didn't think there'd be a rush to make any decisions, but with Scarlett watching his every move, he couldn't afford to let the ball drop on anything.

"Did Aunt Sadie tell you that I didn't do any lessons yesterday?"

"No." Reid had figured it out after the twins talked about spending the whole day goofing off with her. "I think we should take a tour of the middle school and see about enrolling you."

"I like being homeschooled."

"You don't have anyone to take on the responsibility of managing your studies."

"Can't you?"

"I'll be too busy once I find a job."

"Aunt Sadie can help me."

"She's got the twins to take care of and all of the ranch finances."

Jessie's chin jutted. "Then Grandpa can do it."

If his grandfather was in charge of Jessie's studies, they'd be playing internet poker all day.

"It doesn't matter, because I'm on spring break right now," Jessie said.

"Spring break?"

"Tommy and Tyler are on spring break so I decided to take one, too."

He wondered what Scarlett thought of that.

Jessie walked over to the cleaning supplies on the counter. "I can help."

She was trying to get on his good side, hoping he'd drop the subject. He let her win this round. "You could clean all the windows."

"Okay."

Reid opened the box with the pub table and began assembling the pieces. He and Jessie had been working for over half an hour when she said, "I'm sorry I was mean about the dog crate."

Reid set the screwdriver down. "I'm sorry, too. I should have discussed buying the pet carrier with you first."

Jessie glanced at Fang, who was curled up in a ball inside an overturned box.

"The twins feed Fang at the dinner table and Sadie gets irritated when the boys don't eat their supper." Reid stood. "Maybe at mealtimes the dog could stay in the carrier and then afterward you could let the boys feed him a few table scraps."

She nodded.

"When we move in here," he said, "Fang can use the crate as a bed if he gets cold during the day."

Jessie went back to cleaning windows and Reid finished putting the table together, then checked on Jessie's progress. "Nice job. I can see out of them." She smiled, and a tiny bit of the fear inside Reid receded. "I think we're done for the night." He collected the cooler and waited by the door.

"Can we bring the carrier back to the house in case Fang wants to sleep in it?" she asked.

"Sure." He grabbed the crate and she picked up the dog.

"Thank you for thinking of him."

Keeping a straight face he said, "If you want a place to hide from the twins, I can buy you a kennel, too."

Jessie giggled. "Ha. Ha."

Reid locked the cabin door and neither of them talked during the drive back to the main house, but Reid didn't mind because he and Jessie had made progress tonight—a few steps forward in the right direction.

Chapter Seven

"Don't get mad at me but I swear little Amelia looks like Gunner," Scarlett stared at the sleeping baby snuggled in the bassinet in Lydia's living room.

Her cousin pressed a finger against her lips and motioned for Scarlett to follow her into the kitchen. "I have a feeling I'll be buying denim rompers and kiddie cowboy hats instead of pink satin dresses and hair bows."

Scarlett had stopped by Lydia and Gunner's apartment in town after getting off work early Friday afternoon. One of Scarlett's clients had come down with the flu and she'd had to cancel the home visit. When she'd arrived at the apartment she'd discovered Jessie had been dropped off earlier when Sadie took the twins to a birthday party. Jessie had been downstairs in Lydia's office most of the day playing games on her laptop.

"Did Jessie leave Fang at the ranch?"

Lydia nodded. "He's in his dog carrier. Sadie said she'd let him out when she returned from the birthday party."

"Why hasn't Reid picked her up before now?"

"He took Emmett and Amelia into San Antonio to meet with a carnival company. The rodeo and festival is only three weeks away."

Scarlett was growing concerned that Reid wasn't making Jessie a priority. She understood the rodeo was important but if she didn't hear from Reid on a decision about his daughter's education by Monday, she'd have to schedule an *official* home visit at the cabin.

"When are your parents coming to see the baby?"

"They keep changing the date. First, it was next week, then last night they phoned and said the week after and this morning I got a text saying it would be a month from now." She brushed a strand of hair out of her tired face. "I wouldn't be surprised if they re-schedule again."

Lydia's parents were partners in a law firm in Madison and their careers had always come before family. Her cousin poured two glasses of iced tea and brought them to the table.

"It smells heavenly in here. What are you baking?"

"Brownies."

Scarlett took a sip of tea. "I've been lax about looking for an apartment since moving here. I need to step up my game."

"There's no rush. Sadie and the boys love having you at the ranch."

But there was a rush, because as soon as she closed Jessie's case, she wanted to get back to where she and her client's father had left off. Staring at those blue eyes across the dinner table from her had been pure torture. "Last night Emmett and Aunt Amelia went at it again over dessert. They bicker about every little thing."

"That's nothing new."

"I asked Emmett if he wanted his bedroom back, but he changed the subject." Scarlett smiled. "I think he likes staying at Amelia's. She probably spoils him."

Scarlett laughed.

"I told Gunner the other day that when Emmett finally admits he loves Aunt Amelia, she'll stop trying to change Stampede."

"If Reid's handling the rodeo, who's organizing the festival?" Scarlett asked.

"Supposedly you, me and Sadie." The oven timer dinged and Lydia removed the pan of brownies. "I'm having a bunch of flyers printed up to distribute. They should be here next Monday or Tuesday." Lydia grabbed three dessert plates from the cupboard and forks from the silverware drawer.

"I don't know how Aunt Amelia will pull this off in three weeks."

"If you have enough money you can accomplish anything." Lydia lowered her voice. "Is there anything going on between you and Reid?"

"No, why would you ask that?" Had Reid told his brothers he'd kissed her?

"Sadie says you two do a lot of staring into each other's eyes at the dinner table." Lydia squeezed Scarlett's hand. "It hasn't been that long since your relationship with Dale ended."

Her cousins believed Scarlett had moved to Texas to get over a broken heart, not because she'd been forced to resign from her job.

"There's nothing going on between us," Scarlett said. But she wished there was because trying to ignore her growing attraction to Reid was more challenging than she'd anticipated. "You're one to talk about rushing things."

Lydia's eyes widened. "What do mean?"

"You had a fling with Gunner and if you hadn't ended up pregnant, you might not have married him."

"At the time I thought that, too, but looking back—" Lydia smiled. "Gunner had me at 'dairyland princess.'"

"What?"

"When I walked into the motel, he took one look at me and said—" Lydia deepened her voice "—'If it isn't the dairyland princess.'"

"Can I come up?" Jessie hollered from the first floor.

Lydia walked over to the stairs. "You sure can."

Jessie entered the kitchen and asked, "Did you bake something?"

"Brownies." Lydia cut the dessert into several large squares, then dished out three servings and added a scoop of ice cream on each plate.

"These are good," Jessie said.

"I appreciate the compliment—" Lydia winked "—but they came out of a box."

"My mom made cakes from box mixes," Jessie said.

Lydia offered a sympathetic smile. "It's been hectic with the baby coming right when you and your father arrived in town. I've been meaning to tell you how sorry I am that you lost your mother."

Jessie nodded, but kept her eyes on the plate.

"What's your favorite subject in school?" Scarlett asked, changing the subject.

"I like math," Jessie said.

"That's fabulous." Lydia pointed her fork. "Have you thought about what you might like to study in college?"

Jessie glanced between the women. "College?"

"You are planning to go to college, aren't you?" Lydia poured Jessie a glass of milk.

"My mom didn't go to college." She gulped the milk.

"That's because she had to take care of you," Scarlett said. How different things might have turned out for Stacy if she'd told Reid about their child. He might have insisted they marry and Stacy would have lived on base housing while Reid served in Afghanistan. She might even have gone to college part-time. At the very least, Scarlett knew Reid would have supported her financially. But because she'd kept Jessie a secret, she not only shortchanged her daughter and Reid, she'd shortchanged herself.

Jessie looked at Scarlett. "Did you have to go to college to be a social worker?"

Scarlett nodded. "If you like math you could study engineering. The workforce needs more females in those types of jobs."

"What does an engineer do?" Jessie asked.

"They use math, science and technology to solve problems." Scarlett set her fork on the plate. "You could get a job in the medical field or work with computers and machines."

Lydia carried her plate to the sink, then went to check on the baby in the other room.

"Engineers make good money," Scarlett said.

"Me and my mom never went on vacations because she said we didn't have enough money."

"As an engineer you'd make enough money to take a few vacations every year," Scarlett said.

"If I want to go to college, would I have to go to a real school?"

"You mean a public school?"

Jessie nodded.

"Not necessarily."

"My dad said I have to go to a public school because he doesn't have the time to help me with my classes."

This was why she needed to talk with Reid. He was making decisions for Jessie without having all the facts. "Parents don't have to be the ones to homeschool their kids."

"I told him that Aunt Sadie or Grandpa could help, but he said they were too busy."

Scarlett tapped a nail against the tabletop. If Reid pushed his daughter into something she didn't want to do or wasn't ready to do, Jessie could decide she didn't want to live with him after all. "If you feel strongly about wanting to continue with your homeschooling you need to tell your father and then I'll help you locate a program coordinator who will monitor your studies."

Jessie's face lit up. "Really?"

"Really." Scarlett smiled. "How does Fang like his the pet carrier?"

"He likes it." Jessie pushed her empty plate away. "Grandpa gave me a blanket to put inside it."

"That's nice."

Jessie glanced over her shoulder, then whispered, "Do my uncles like my dad?"

Scarlett kept her eyes on Jessie, but she saw Lydia peek through the doorway.

"Of course your uncles like your father."

"They don't act like they do."

"What do you mean?" Scarlett asked.

"They hardly talk to each other and my dad never does anything with them."

"You've only been at the ranch a week. It's a busy place. I'm sure he'll spend more time with your uncles soon."

"My mom said she left home because her parents kicked her out when she told them she got pregnant with me."

"That's rough." Unfortunately Scarlett had worked with pregnant teens whose parents had been just as heartless.

Scarlett reached across the table and clasped Jessie's hand. "When people are separated from their family for long periods of time, it takes a while for everyone to settle in with each other. Don't worry. You and your dad will always be part of this family."

Jessie shook her head. "I bet we don't stay here."

"Do you want to make Stampede your home?"

"This place is okay, I guess."

"There's not much for girls your age to do in this small town."

"I like the petting zoo. Grandpa says I'm a big help because I can keep an eye on Tommy and Tyler."

"The twins are a handful."

"Scarlett, does my grandpa like that old lady?"

"You mean Aunt Amelia?"

Jessie nodded.

"They used to date in high school."

"Does she have any grandkids?"

Scarlett shook her head. "Aunt Amelia never had any children of her own."

"I guess I wouldn't mind living here if they let my dad stay."

Was Reid aware that his daughter was worried about being able to remain in town? He needed to show Scarlett that he was doing everything in his power to provide Jessie with a sense of security before he petitioned for permanent custody. She took their plates to the sink. "Have you seen Stampede's library yet?"

"No."

"Let's thank Lydia for the brownies, then we'll walk over and check out the bookshelves."

THIS IS A waste of time and money." Emmett glanced over his shoulder and glared at Amelia in the back seat.

Reid kept his attention on the road and pressed his foot harder on the gas. The old couple had been sparring since they'd left town a half hour ago. He'd have thought a pair of eighty-five-year-olds would have better things to do with their time than keep up a steady stream of bickering.

"It's my money to waste," Amelia said. "And in case you haven't looked in the mirror lately, you and I don't have a lot of time left before we park ourselves in front of the pearly gates."

Emmett waved a hand. "First she runs roughshod over me and fixes up the motel and then—"

"The motel looks nice, Gramps. I bet Grandma's smiling in heaven." The comment shut his grandfather up because he knew Sara Hardell had loved the Moonlight.

"Don't forget to take exit 141C," Amelia said.

"I admit the motel looks a heap better with new paint slapped on it, but—"

"Slapped on it?" Amelia snorted. "Lydia put a lot of thought and hard work into renovating the property."

"You could have stopped with the motel, but you had to turn my ranch into a zoological garden and add that blasted death march at the back of the property for fancy-pants urban cowboys."

Jeez. When had the old man become so melodramatic?

"Paradise Ranch is doing better financially. Stop complaining," she said.

His grandfather should be grateful the back seat driver had been generous with her dead husband's money.

"Your grandfather wouldn't be happy if he didn't have something to gripe about," Amelia said. "Do you know he complained after I let him kiss me on our first date in high school?"

The old man looked as if he'd applied lady's blush to his cheeks. "Wasn't much of a kiss."

Amelia reached over the seat and whacked Emmett's arm. "I let you kiss me on the lips and that's more than most girls did back in the day."

Reid took the next exit and got off the freeway. "What time is your appointment with the carnival company?"

Emmett pointed his thumb over his shoulder. "Ask the boss."

"Noon," Amelia said. "I thought afterward we could stop for a bite to eat at the Cracker Barrel. That's your grandfather's favorite restaurant."

"That's the best idea you've had in months," Emmett said.

"My cheesy hash-brown casserole is better than the Cracker Barrel recipe."

"How come you haven't made it for me?" Emmett asked.

"Because you're always down at the café drinking coffee with your cronies before I crawl out of bed in the morning."

Emmett nudged Reid's arm. "She's a pampered princess."

"And whose fault is that?" she asked. "Reid, did you know that your grandfather sets out my teacup in the morning before he leaves the house?"

"Ain't hard to take a cup out of the cupboard."

"Emmett doesn't like other people to know that underneath all that bluster, he's a true gentlemen."

Maybe dementia was setting in with these two, because Reid didn't recall his grandfather ever practicing good manners.

"Sara once told me that on your grandparents' first wedding anniversary Emmett cut a bouquet of roses from the bushes in front of the house and placed them on the pillow next to her while she slept."

Reid exchanged an amused smile with his grandfather. His grandma hadn't told her best friend the whole story. She'd left out the part where she'd woken up to ants crawling all over her. She'd run shrieking down the hall to the bathroom where she'd jumped in the shower with her nightgown on.

Reid turned right on Fifth Street and drove past a handful of warehouses. "Here we are." He pulled into the lot of A&B Attractions and parked by the door marked Office.

They piled out of the pickup, Emmett opening the back door for Amelia and offering her his hand as she stepped down. "We don't need more than a couple of rides," he said.

"We'll see."

Gramps looked at Reid. "'We'll see' is code for 'I'm ignoring you.'"

Reid ushered the couple inside where a stout man

with gray sideburns greeted them. "You must be Ms. Amelia Rinehart and Emmett Hardell." He waved them to the chairs in front of his desk. Reid signaled that he'd stand against the wall at the back of the room.

"Reginald Humphrey at your service," the man said. "How might A&B Attractions serve your community?"

"We're in need of rides and gaming booths for a carnival in three weeks," Amelia said.

The sideburns moved forward when Mr. Humphrey pursed his lips. "You're getting a late start."

Amelia glared at Emmett. "That's his fault."

Reid jumped into the conversation and ended the bickering war before it began. "There's only room for three or four rides on the property," he said. "And a few game booths."

"The smallest show we take on the road is six rides and four booths." Humphrey rubbed his chin. "I wouldn't be able to send you the popular rides, but I could throw in a fortune teller."

"That would be fun," Amelia said. "Do you provide food venders?"

"We do." Humphrey removed a brochure from the desk drawer. "I recommend the corn dog stand, which also sells burgers. The fry bread truck is popular and of course you'll also want the cotton candy and kettle corn stand. Those also sell drinks."

Amelia looked at Emmett. "Lydia says there's room behind the motel for three or four food trucks."

"How many days will you need the attraction for?"

"Two. Saturday and Sunday," Amelia said.

"We require a minimum of five days. Anything less and we don't make a profit."

"What do you charge for five days?" Amelia asked.

Mr. Humphrey quoted a substantial amount, then said, "We split the profits sixty-forty with the town."

"How much does that sixty percent usually come out to?" she asked.

"Depends on the location." Humphrey slid on a pair of reading glasses and opened the notepad on the desk. "I've never heard of Stampede, Texas. What's the population?"

"Under five thousand," Amelia said.

Way under, but Reid kept his mouth closed.

"We're near the towns of Rocky Point and Mesquite, so we'll draw people from both those areas," Amelia said.

"In order to make it profitable for my company, I'd have to charge more up front for the rental of the rides and food trucks." He threw out a number that Reid suspected was three times the normal price.

Amelia didn't bat an eye. "That will be fine." Emmett's eyes bulged but she ignored him and opened her purse. "Will you take a personal check?"

"Yes, ma'am, I will."

"I'll pay half now and the rest after the rides are set up and running." She wrote out a draft and slid it across the desk. "I included a small bonus. Take your wife out for a nice dinner tonight."

Humphrey's face lit up. "Let me print off a contract and we'll get down to business."

"How long's this gonna take?" Emmett asked.

Humphrey pointed to a door on the other side of the room. "You're welcome to look at the rides in the warehouse while we take care of the paperwork."

Amelia sent Reid a silent message to get Emmett out of the office. "C'mon, Gramps. I'll go with you." He held the door open and followed his grandfather into an enormous warehouse that resembled an airplane hangar. They meandered between the rides, neither speaking. Then his grandfather stopped at the Tilt-a-Whirl and said, "You ready to talk about why you waited so long to come home?"

If his grandfather had been oblivious to what was going on beneath his nose all those years ago, then he'd never believe Reid's version of events so why bother. "I'd rather not talk about it."

His grandfather opened his mouth, no doubt to argue, but Amelia's voice rang out, saving Reid from a grilling.

"Where are you, Emmett?"

The old man grasped Reid's shirtsleeve. "Out of all the boys you were the one who didn't need to be reined in. Sara and I never had to worry about you toeing the line."

If his grandfather had bothered to look closer, he might have figured out why Reid hadn't made waves—because he hadn't wanted to give his father more reasons to pick on him. "If you want to eat at Cracker Barrel, we'd better get on the road."

Chapter Eight

Scarlett knocked on the cabin door late Monday afternoon. She and Reid were scheduled to meet about Jessie tomorrow morning, but he'd left a voice mail on her phone asking her to stop by as soon as she got off work.

"Come in." Reid turned away from the fridge where he'd been loading a case of water bottles and smiled.

"Wow. You've gotten a lot done in the ten days since you arrived in town." Yes, she was keeping track of the days. Reid had checked out of his motel room this past Thursday night and officially moved into the cabin, but Jessie still slept on the couch at the main house. It was Scarlett's responsibility to keep the pair moving forward on the right track.

His gaze roamed over her, stalling for a fraction of a second on her breasts before returning to her face, where her cheeks were growing warmer by the second.

It was a challenge to stay focused in Reid's presence. The old adage *you always want what you can't have* popped into her head. Whenever they were anywhere near each other, her hormones went crazy.

"You got my voice mail," he said.

The message—*we need to talk about Jessie*—had been vague, but there was no mistaking the careful tone in his voice. "I did." She brushed her hand over the gray sofa cushions. "Did Jessie help pick this out?"

"Your aunt bought all the furniture and had it delivered to the cabin. Payment for helping her with the rodeo."

Scarlett drew in a deep breath and faced Reid. He'd struck a sexy pose—crossing his arms over his chest and leaning a hip against the counter. "What is it you wanted to discuss with me that couldn't wait until our meeting tomorrow?"

"Why did you tell Jessie she could continue with her homeschooling program?"

"Jessie said you wanted her to enroll in a public school because there was no one to monitor her studies. I told her that wasn't true. That I could help her find a qualified instructor to track her progress."

"But I didn't ask for your help."

She bristled. "You didn't need to. It's my job to step in and handle things that come up like this."

"You should have talked to me before you made a promise like that to Jessie."

They locked gazes. "What's really bothering you?" she asked.

The muscle in his jaw ticked. "I'm Jessie's father. Isn't it my right to decide what's best for her?"

"If it's money you're worried about—"

"It's not about the money." He shoved away from the counter and walked outside. Scarlett followed, stopping in the doorway when she saw his clenched fists.

"Is this how it works?" He turned.

"What do you mean?"

"If I make a decision for Jessie that you don't agree with, you rein me in?"

"Why are you against homeschooling?"

"Why are you against public schools?" he asked.

"This isn't about me, Reid. This is about what's best for your daughter."

"Maybe I know what's best for her."

"Jessie said she wanted to be homeschooled, but you told her she couldn't, because there was no one to teach her. So I stepped in and solved the problem. I don't understand why you're upset."

"Let me get this straight," he said. "I have to give her everything she wants, or I'm a bad parent?"

He was twisting her words. "Do you even know why she wants to stay in a homeschool program?"

He looked away. "Did she tell you why?"

"No. You're her father. You need to ask her." She drew in a deep breath. "Before you make decisions for Jessie, it's important to understand what she's thinking and where she's coming from."

His gaze connected with hers and the uncertainty in his eyes tugged at her heart. She grasped his arm, her fingers flexing against the muscle. He looked so miserable she wanted to hug him. "It's okay. Parents aren't perfect."

He stared at her hand, then his eyes shifted to her face and the bleakness she'd seen in his stare moments ago was replaced by a warm glow. Alarms went off in her brain, but when he focused his attention on her mouth, her lashes fluttered closed. Reid's lips brushed across hers and she sighed, releasing all the pent-up desire in her. Her arms had a will of their own and she curled them around his neck, moaning when he grasped her face and tilted her head, giving him better access to her mouth. The calluses on the palms of his hands created a delicious friction against her skin and she shivered when she imagined his fingers sliding over her thighs…her stomach…her…

His hand cupped her breast, startling Scarlett and she jumped back. "I'm sorry." Legs shaking, she skipped down the steps and raced to her car. She opened the driver's-side door, then said, "That shouldn't have happened." She got into the vehicle and it took all of her willpower not to glance at Reid as she drove off.

"GOOD MORNING, REID," Sadie said when he stepped into the kitchen Tuesday and found the twins and Jessie eating pancakes at the table.

"'Morning." He glanced at the floor, looking for the dog. "Where's Fang?"

"In his crate." Tommy pointed to the pet carrier sitting in the laundry-room doorway. The mutt was curled up on his blanket snoozing.

"Help yourself." Sadie nodded to the coffee maker on the counter. "I'll have another batch of pancakes ready in a minute."

Reid filled a mug, then joined the kids at the table. "What do you boys have planned today?"

"We gotta go to school," Tyler said.

"I forgot spring break is over." Reid sipped his coffee. "Do you two have the same teacher?"

Their heads bobbed.

"According to the boys, Mrs. McGowan looks like this." Sadie set a plate in front of Reid and the boys giggled at the pancake face—beady blueberry eyes with angry whipped eyebrows, a frowning banana mouth and a shriveled raisin nose.

"Yikes," Reid said.

"Mrs. McGowan doesn't like to smile." Tommy looked at his brother. "Right?"

Tyler nodded.

"Finish eating." Sadie pointed at the hallway off the kitchen. "I just heard the front door open, and you know what that means."

Jessie nudged Reid's arm. "Grandpa drives them to the school bus."

Reid shoveled a bite of Mrs. McGowan into his mouth. "Me, your uncle Logan and your uncle Gunner had to walk to the bus every day."

The twins exchanged glances, then Tommy asked, "Can we walk to the bus, Mom?"

Sadie topped off Reid's mug and gave him the evil eye.

"Actually," he said. "I think it was only one time we had to walk to the bus stop, because Grandpa's truck broke down."

"Let's go, rascals," Emmett hollered from the foyer.

"Don't forget your backpacks are by the door," Sadie shouted after the twins left the room.

Footsteps sounded in the hallway and Tyler raced back into the kitchen to give his mother a hug, then he stopped by Jessie's chair and gave her a squeeze before running outside.

"Tyler has a crush on you." Sadie smiled. "Ever since you told him you love to read, he thinks you're as cool as Superman and Captain America."

"Tyler told me about his secret reading spot," Jessie said.

"Where's that?" Reid asked.

"The loft in the barn," she said. "Uncle Logan made

this cool chair out of hay and Tyler likes to sit up there and read."

His older brother surprised Reid. Logan hadn't been the twins' father for a full year and yet he knew exactly how to impress them. And here Reid sat at the table with his biological daughter who still felt like someone else's kid and not his own.

He looked at Jessie. "I thought we'd go on a trail ride this morning."

"Uncle Logan offered to take me tomorrow."

Great. It wouldn't help his cause if Scarlett found out Jessie was spending time with her uncle and not her father.

Sadie winked at Reid. "Logan forgot to tell you, Jessie. He has an appointment in Rocky Point tomorrow."

"Then it looks like we can go," Reid said.

"If you'll excuse me, I need to make a call." Sadie left the kitchen and Reid heard the office door close. He suspected his sister-in-law was phoning Logan about his plans with Jessie.

"Can we call Scarlett and see if she wants to come along?" Jessie asked.

"Scarlett's at work. I thought it would be nice for just the two of us to spend time together." He and Jessie needed to come to an agreement on the school issue and, more important, he wanted Jessie to understand that he was her guardian, not Scarlett. "Ready?"

"What about Fang? Can I bring him if he rides in my backpack?"

Reid opened his mouth to say the dog should stay in the house, then thought better of it. Fang was Jessie's security blanket and she might need the Chihuahua after their talk. "Sure." He took his dishes to the sink and poured the remainder of his coffee down the drain. "I'll wait outside. Don't forget a jacket."

Jessie left the house a few minutes later, carrying a cloth knapsack and wearing a hooded sweatshirt. Fang was dressed in his Superman doggy shirt. Once she buckled up, Reid drove off, thinking they might pass his grandfather's pickup on the way to the highway, but the old man must have driven into town after making sure the boys had boarded the bus.

"Do you like Scarlett?" Jessie asked.

"Yeah. She's a nice lady." A nice lady who he wished wasn't a social worker right now.

Jessie peeked at him, then looked away. "I meant like a girlfriend."

He squirmed in his seat, worried he'd given off signals that he was attracted to his daughter's caseworker. "Of course not."

"Did you have a girlfriend before you found out about me?"

What was happening here? He should be directing the conversation. "I dated a woman for a little while. It wasn't serious."

"Was she mad when you moved to Texas to see me?"

He shook his head. "No, we'd broken up by then." Enough talk about him. "Have you ever ridden a horse before?" There was still so much he didn't know about his daughter even after the six months of supervised visits in El Paso.

"My mom took me to a carnival when I was little and I rode a pony like Ruby." She glanced across the seat. "Did you rodeo like Uncle Logan and Uncle Gunner?"

"A few times. I wasn't very good." He'd turned eighteen at the beginning of his senior year of high school and had entered a handful of saddle-bronc competitions but hadn't done well.

"Is that where you met my mom? At a rodeo?"

"No. Your mom was at a graduation party with a group of friends when I saw her."

"She told me she was older than you and stuff."

He couldn't remember if he and Stacy had mentioned their ages. By *stuff* he suspected Jessie was referring to him and her mother making out.

"I'm only twelve but I know how babies are made. How could you get naked with my mom and then not want to see her again?"

He glanced across the seat. "Is that what she told you?"

Jessie nodded.

Shock spread through Reid, then a few seconds later surprise gave way to anger. If Stacy had contacted him, he wouldn't have turned his back on her and he would have done his best to maintain a relationship with his daughter. No wonder Jessie had been so nervous when they'd first met in El Paso—she thought he hadn't cared about her. "I'm sorry she told you that," he said, "but I never knew I'd gotten your mother pregnant."

Jessie gathered Fang closer, probably wondering whether he was lying or not. "Why didn't my mom tell you?"

It wouldn't have been that difficult for Stacy to track him down, if she'd really wanted to. He'd told her about enlisting in the marines and obviously she'd remembered his last name, because he'd been listed as the father on Jessie's birth certificate. Reid had no idea why Stacy would lie to their daughter, but she wasn't here to defend herself. And because she had raised Jessie with no help from family, he'd cut her some slack.

"Your mom might have thought I didn't want anything to do with you because I didn't give her my phone number the night we met."

"Why not?"

"I was leaving town for boot camp a few days later." He drew in a quiet breath, wondering if he should just shut up or keep talking. "After I left the military, I didn't come back to Texas, so I doubt your mom could have found me."

Stacy should have reached out to his family, but Jessie would come to that conclusion on her own as she grew older.

"If you had known about me, would you have tried to see me?"

"I'd have made an effort to not only visit you but to be part of your life." He turned onto the road, which led to the riding stables. Logan's pickup was gone, but there were two horses saddled in the corral—one with a child's riding helmet tied to a stirrup that had been adjusted for Jessie's shorter legs.

Reid trusted that Logan had handpicked a gentle horse for his niece and appreciated his brother's thoughtfulness. He parked next to the corral. Jessie attached the leash to Fang's collar and then let the dog pee before putting him inside the knapsack and zipping it until only his head poked through the top.

"Wait here." He went into the corral and walked Jessie's horse out. "This one is yours."

"Does it have a name?"

"I'm sure she does, but you'll have to ask your uncle at dinner tonight." He helped Jessie adjust the strap on the riding helmet, then cupped his hands next to the stirrup. "I'll give you a boost." She grasped his shoulders, then he lifted her into the air and she swung her leg over the mare. "Be careful that you don't jerk the reins."

"Why?" she asked.

"The horse might spook and you and Fang could fall."

"I'll be careful."

He knew she would, because she didn't want anything to happen to the dog. Reid mounted his horse and then clicked his tongue and the pair walked over to the entrance to the trail.

"Where are we going?" she asked.

"Past this rock formation."

"What's on the other side?"

"A neighboring ranch." Reid was impressed with the trail, which was wide enough for three horses side by side.

They rode in silence for a while, then Reid brought up the subject of Jessie's schooling. "Scarlett told me she could find someone to monitor your homeschooling, so you don't have to go to the middle school in Mesquite. I didn't know we had other options." He waited until they climbed a small hill, then he said, "I'm open to letting you continue with your homeschooling program, but I think you owe it to yourself to take a tour of middle school, then decide which is best for you."

"I know what's best for me. I like homeschooling."

Obviously his daughter inherited her stubbornness from him. "Have you ever attended a public school?"

Jessie took so long to answer he thought she'd forgotten he'd asked the question. "My mom dated my fourth-grade teacher. Mr. Koppel was supposed to marry my mom and we were gonna live in his house."

Reid remained quiet, letting Jessie tell the story in her own time.

"But then my mom came home after going to a movie with Mr. Koppel and she was crying. The next day at school Mrs. Cleaver called me to the principal's office and said I couldn't be in Mr. Koppel's class anymore. I ask Mr. Koppel why, and he said it was because he broke up with my mom. I told him I didn't care. I still wanted to stay in his class, but he made me go to Mrs. Lane's room."

Reid could imagine how difficult that situation had been for Jessie.

"When Mom came home from work I told her what happened and she called Mr. Koppel and yelled at him on the phone. In the morning she took me to school and told the principal that I wasn't coming back." Jessie looked at Reid and the tears in her eyes sucker-punched him in the gut. "My mom said she'd homeschool me and then we moved to an apartment close to her job and I never saw any of my friends again."

"I'm sorry, Jessie."

She wiped a tear from her eyes and sniffed. "Mr. Koppel said he was going to be my dad but he changed his mind and then he kicked me out of his class."

Reid sided with his daughter. How could her teacher have been so insensitive? No wonder Jessie kept her guard up—she didn't trust Reid not to walk out on her, too. There was nothing he could do or say to change the past or make the hurt go away, but now he understood why Jessie was hesitant to attend a public school. And maybe that's why she was dragging her feet about moving into the cabin—she worried Reid might change his mind and walk away from her, too.

"I bet you missed your friends," he said.

She nodded.

"If you went to a public school you'd have a chance to make new friends." She didn't say anything. "Think about taking a tour and I'll tell Scarlett to be on the lookout for an advisor to help homeschool you." Time to drop the subject.

"You know you're welcome to sleep at the cabin now," he said.

Jessie nodded.

"I bought Fang a bag of dog food and some toys so when you're ready to use your bedroom, the cabin will feel like his home, too."

She remained quiet.

"Have you given any thought to where you might want to spread your mother's ashes?" His daughter had put the urn on the fireplace mantel in the living room at the main house.

"Are we gonna stay here forever?" Jessie asked.

"I don't know," he said. "You're used to the city. Do you like living in the country?"

"I like all the animals. And I don't mind Tommy and Tyler bugging me."

The ranch was beginning to feel like home to his daughter and Reid was feeling pressure to make the situation work. "Whether we stay or not depends on what kind of job I can find."

"Can't you help Uncle Logan with the ranch? Or Uncle Gunner with the motel?"

He doubted his brothers wanted him invading their

territory. "I'm going to look for work as a mechanic in Rocky Point or Mesquite."

"Would we have to move there?"

"Nope. We'd live in the cabin and I'd commute."

"I think I want to stay here then," she said.

"I hope that means you'll move into the cabin soon. I'm lonely out there all by myself."

"Tommy and Tyler won't like me leaving."

"They'll get used to it."

"I think my mom would like it if I spread her ashes here," Jessie said.

"By the cabin?"

She shook her head. "Grandpa said he put Grandma Sara's ashes by a stream and a bunch of daisies."

"I know the spot he's talking about."

"Will you take me there sometime, so I can see if I like it?"

"Sure." If Jessie had her heart set on making Paradise Ranch their forever home, then Reid needed to clear the air with his brothers.

"Can we do this again?" Jessie asked.

"You mean go for a horseback ride?"

"Or something else if you want," she said.

"I'd like that." The knot that had formed in his chest when he'd loaded Jessie's things into his pickup and had driven away from the Valentines' home in El Paso was slowly unraveling.

Chapter Nine

"Where is everyone?" Reid asked when he entered the kitchen Saturday afternoon and found his grandfather peeling potatoes at the sink.

"Shopping in San Antonio. They should be back by suppertime."

"Did Jessie go, too?"

His grandfather glanced over his shoulder. "She didn't tell you?"

Reid shook his head.

"Did you check your phone messages? Scarlett told her to ask you."

Reid pulled his phone from his back pocket and saw the text from his daughter. "I forgot I turned off my cell."

"What for?"

"I drove into Mesquite to talk to an auto body shop about a job."

"Did they hire you?"

Reid took a water bottle out of the fridge and sat at the table. "They offered me the job, but I turned it down."

"Why?"

"They didn't mention in their job posting that it was

part-time and weekends." He wanted a nine-to-five position with Saturday and Sunday off so he could do things with Jessie. He doubted a judge would look favorably upon him if he didn't spend time with his daughter when she wasn't in school.

"You still planning on riding in the rodeo?" Gramps asked.

"Yeah, why?"

"Your brothers are practicing in the corral right now." He grinned at Reid. "The rodeo is two weeks away. You might want to get out there and go a couple of rounds so you don't embarrass yourself."

Reid left the house and cut across the yard. When he reached the fence, he sat on the top rail and took in the show.

A mechanical bull had been placed in the middle of the corral, surrounded by old mattresses. "Did you go Dumpster diving for those things?" he called out. When they'd been kids Logan and Gunner would dig through the trash behind the motel, looking for "treasures" the guests had accidently thrown out.

"I kept a few of the mattresses from the Moonlight after Lydia renovated the rooms," Gunner said.

"You and Jessie settled in now?" Logan asked.

Reid nodded. "You're welcome to stop by the cabin and check it out."

Logan walked over to Reid. "Jessie told Sadie the other day that you two are definitely staying in Stampede."

"I went into Mesquite to see about a job but it was part-time."

"I can put a few feelers out," Logan said. "What kind of work are you looking for?"

Reid lifted his hands. "I'd like to stick to what I know. Engines."

"Smart decision." Logan grinned. "You suck at rodeo."

Reid chuckled. "We can't all be as good as you."

His brother's expression grew sober. "You could have picked up a thing or two from watching me, if you'd have come to my rodeos back in high school."

Reid bristled. "Someone had to do the chores when you took off all the time."

"Reid was always a Goody Two-shoes." Gunner swung on top of the machine and pointed to the control box. "Hit level one. I need to stretch out my back." Logan picked up the remote control and the mechanical bull rose and lowered like an ocean wave.

"You're real funny, Gunner." Reid had come out here with the best of intentions but leave it to his brothers to poke and prod him. "Like you don't know why I was always toeing the line."

Logan moved the switch and bull jerked to a stop, tossing Gunner onto the mattresses. He scrambled to his feet and walked over to the fence. "What are you talking about?"

"Dad was always harder on me than you two," Reid said.

His brothers exchanged perplexed looks and then Logan asked, "What are you talking about?"

"You guys never wondered why I missed so many suppers or why I was always left behind when the family went somewhere?" His brothers' blank stares puzzled Reid and the first niggling of doubt crept into his mind.

"I don't know where you get off thinking you had it

tough growing up," Logan said. "I was the one screwing up and getting yelled at by Gramps when I'd forget to do a chore."

"What about Dad? Did he ever yell at you?" Reid asked.

Logan opened his mouth, then closed it and looked at Gunner who said, "I don't remember Dad ever yelling at anyone."

"That's because he never yelled. He was real quiet when he threatened me."

"Threatened you?" Logan snorted. "You must have smoked something over in Afghanistan that screwed with your head."

"Did Dad ever tell you to get out of his sight? Did he call you worthless?"

"Are you saying Dad verbally abused you?" Gunner asked.

When his brothers stared with confused expressions, Reid wondered if maybe his siblings hadn't been aware of how their father had treated the middle son.

"Dad wasn't perfect," Logan said. "We all know he cheated on Mom and drank too much. But I don't remember him singling you out."

"Do you know why I didn't go with the family to the state fair that one year?"

"Dad said you weren't feeling well." Gunner glanced at Reid. "Mom said so, too." He snapped his fingers. "I remember when we got home that night Mom brought you a piece of chocolate cake at bedtime, because she felt sorry for you."

"That wasn't why she felt sorry for me." Reid stared at the tips of his boots, hating that after all these years his father's harsh words still hurt. "Dad told me to stay behind because I was a worthless piece of horse crap and he wasn't going to spend any money on me that he didn't have to."

Gunner shook his head. "You're making this up."

"Why do you think when Dad came in from the road I never ate with the family?"

"'Cause you were always wanting to get a jump on your chores, so you didn't have to wake early in the morning." As soon as Gunner spoke, the blood drained from his face. "You didn't sleep in," he said.

"Why didn't you speak up?" Logan paced several feet away and glared. "You never said a damn word, Reid."

"I couldn't. Dad would have come down harder on me if he thought I was bellyaching to you and Gunner." Reid removed his cowboy hat and stared at it. "I had to face Dad all alone." He looked at his brothers. "Because you two never stood up for me."

"Is that why you joined the military?" Gunner asked. Reid nodded.

"And that's why you never came home when you were discharged?" Logan asked. "Because you thought we didn't care about you?"

"What was I supposed to think? That the family missed me?"

The muscle along Logan's jaw bunched and Reid sensed his brother was genuinely distressed to learn their father had mistreated him. "Did he ever hit you?"

"Not with his fist."

"What's that supposed to mean?" Gunner asked.

"Dad was working on his pickup one day and I asked if I could help." Reid shrugged. "He told me to hand him a tool and I gave him the wrong one. He got pissed and yelled at me to get lost. When I turned and walked away, he threw a wrench at me." Reid's back had been sore for a week.

"Why didn't you tell Gramps?" Gunner said.

"Dad threatened to kick me off the ranch if I complained to anyone."

"Shouldn't you boys be practicing instead of jawing like a bunch of gossiping women?" Gramps stood near the fence, his face ashen. He bent down and slipped between the rails and then grabbed an empty feed bucket. He turned it upside down and sat on it. "Guess it's time I told you some truths about your parents."

"What truths?" Reid asked.

"Your grandmother wanted me to tell you boys before she died, but I was having a hard enough time dealing with her illness." The old man rubbed the whiskers on his jaw. "I'd planned to break the news before Reid went to boot camp, but I chickened out. Then Donny died and I didn't think it mattered." He narrowed his eyes on each of his grandsons. "Had I known it was standing between you three all these years, I would have spoken up sooner."

"What are you talking about, Gramps?" Gunner asked.

"Hold your horses. I'm getting there." The old man drew in a ragged breath, then looked at Reid. "Your daddy wasn't your daddy."

Reid flinched as if he'd been punched in the chest and his lungs squeezed so tight, he couldn't get any air in.

"What are you saying, Gramps?" Logan asked.

His brother's voice broke the iron grip on Reid's lungs but the air he sucked in burned his throat.

"Haven't you boys ever wondered why Reid is the only one in the family with blue eyes?"

"Mom and Dad had brown eyes." Gunner pointed at their grandfather. "You have brown eyes and so did Grandma." His brother stared at Reid as if he were a stranger, which was exactly how Reid felt at the moment. He'd never belonged—he wasn't a Hardell. And he hadn't imagined his father's resentment.

"Dad knew, didn't he?" Reid asked.

Gramps nodded.

A kaleidoscope of memories played through his mind, every cruel word and angry glare. Each time he'd laid eyes on Reid, his father had been reminded of his wife's infidelity.

"Is that why Dad stayed away from the ranch for months at a time?" Reid asked.

"Donny and your mother's relationship was never the same after she told him the truth," Gramps said. "Donny didn't handle the news well."

"When did she tell him?" Reid asked.

"I think it was about the time you started school. I can't remember."

He'd been six years old when his dad began hating him. "Is that why Mom left?" Reid asked. "Because Dad couldn't get past her cheating?"

Gramps nodded. "Donny never would forgive her."

Anger lit Reid's nerve endings on fire. "Why didn't Mom take me with her?"

"I wouldn't let her split up you boys."

"How could you do that, Gramps?" Reid choked out.

"We were a family."

Reid shook his head. "No, we weren't." He pointed

to his brothers "You were a family. I was never a part of it."

His grandfather's face blanched.

Reid's pulse pounded so hard he couldn't feel his heart beat. "My father hated my guts and he made sure I knew that every single day he was at the ranch."

His grandfather pulled a cloth from his pocket and wiped his eyes.

Gunner stared at the ground and Logan's fists were clenched at his sides as if he wanted to hit something. "I'm sorry, Reid," Logan said. "We should have paid attention. We should have seen what Dad was doing to you."

"I feel like crap," Gunner said. "Dad used to ask me to go fishing down at the stream and I'd tell him that I wanted Reid to come, too, and he'd say you were busy." Gunner looked miserable. "Dad lied, didn't he?"

Reid nodded.

"You boys aren't to blame for any of this," Gramps said. "You were too young to know what was going on and when you grew into teenagers you were running off in different directions with your friends." He scuffed his toe. "I was dang blasted mad at your father most days, so I steered clear of him." He rubbed his eyes again. "If anyone's to blame, it's me. I left all the up-bringing to your grandmother and tried to ignore what a disappointment Donny was by making myself scare and working sunup to sundown."

"I'm surprised Dad didn't tell Reid himself," Logan said.

"I threatened to throw Donny out of my will if he told Reid."

"Why didn't you share the truth with us after he died?" Reid asked.

"You boys were all off living your own lives. Didn't think it mattered anymore," Gramps said.

"But it did matter." Logan stared at Reid. "You never came home because you thought we didn't care."

Gunner shook his head. "I can't believe Reid's only half a Hardell."

"Stop right there." Gramps pointed a knobby finger. "Reid is every bit a Hardell as you two fools."

"Do you know who my real father is?" Reid asked.

His grandfather's shoulders slumped. "Your mother kept it to herself."

"I'm going for a horseback ride." No one tried to stop him as he walked off. He hopped into his truck and drove with the radio blasting loud enough to drown out the thoughts in his head. When he arrived at the stables, he saddled a horse and took off across the property.

He rode until the wind numbed his face, then he slowed the mare to a walk and finally stopped at a stock tank not far from the hunting cabin. Once the horse drank, he climbed back on and rode the rest of the way to the cabin. He needed time to cool off before he spoke to his brothers and grandfather again. When the cabin came into view, he spotted Scarlett sitting on the porch with a large shopping bag next to her.

Her face lit up when she saw him and the ache that threatened to split his chest open weakened. She was just what he needed to dull the pain. He stopped the horse in front of the steps.

"Sadie dropped me off before she drove the kids back to the house." She pointed to the bag. "Jessie picked out some new linens and I told her I'd fix up her bed for her."

Reid slid off the horse and tied the reins to the porch rail.

"Don't get mad," she said. "Sadie and Lydia paid for the bedding. They wanted to get Jessie a welcome-to-the-family gift."

Reid climbed the steps and Scarlett stood. There was a hair sticking up on the side of her head and he smoothed the silky strand back into place.

"What's the matter?" she asked. "You're acting weird."

After learning the truth about his father, Reid needed confirmation that he mattered. That he had value. That he wasn't worthless. Scarlett was the only person he'd met who'd made him feel important. He brushed his mouth over hers, groaning when her lips parted.

After the kiss ended he cupped her cheek and gazed into her eyes. "Come inside with me." He was asking her to cross the line she'd drawn for their relationship. He held her gaze, allowing her to see the pain in his soul. Scarlett was his anchor and never more than now did he need her to hold him steady.

She threaded her fingers through his and they entered the cabin. He closed the door, then backed her up against the wall and pressed soft kisses over her face.

He wanted to share what he'd learned about his father with her but for now he just needed to hold her. When they came up for air, he waited, giving her one last chance to change her mind.

He hadn't known he'd stopped breathing until her fingers slid inside the belt loop on his jeans. He exhaled, his breath blowing her hair out of place. She led him down the hallway and into his bedroom. He closed the door, then scooped her into his arms and carried her to the bed, laying her down gently.

"You're so beautiful." He nuzzled her throat and her back arched off the mattress. He nibbled her ear before capturing her lips again. When she pressed her body into his, the hurt and anger evaporated and Scarlett's warmth and beauty seeped into his soul. Clothes fell to the floor, then he leaned over her and gazed into her eyes. "I can't get enough of you."

She curled her leg over the back of his thigh and smiled. "Better?"

Reid gave himself over to Scarlett, and she slipped quietly past his defenses and deep into his heart.

SCARLETT RAN HER fingers over Reid's muscular chest, listening to his heavy breathing return to normal. She'd dreamed of making love with him ever since their first kiss years ago. She wasn't panicking about this slipup, and she'd make sure Reid understood this couldn't happen again. But for now she intended to enjoy this moment with him.

There were a lot of parallels between the situation with Reid and Jessie and Dale and Amy but not between the men themselves. Reid wasn't deceitful. Unlike Dale, Reid was still struggling to find his way as his daughter's father. He might not be perfect, but Reid was genuine and sincere—a better man by far than Dale could ever hope to be. She snuggled closer and walked her fingers across his washboard stomach.

Reid trapped her hand when her nail dipped inside his belly button. "I'm not who you think I am."

"What do you mean?" she asked.

"My grandfather dropped a bombshell on me this afternoon."

Scarlett raised her head. "What?"

Reid ran his fingers through Scarlett's short locks, wishing that she didn't have to go back to being Jessie's social worker once they left his bedroom. He just wanted her to be the woman he was falling in love with. He kissed her, pouring his heart into the embrace, needing her to know how important she was to him. When they drew apart, he said, "Donny Hardell isn't my father."

Scarlett sucked in a quick breath. "Has everyone known this but you all these years?"

"My brothers didn't know."

"Now it makes sense why you're the only one with sexy blue eyes." She kissed his eyelids, then rested her cheek on his chest.

"I never came back to Paradise Ranch after I got out of the military because this place had never felt like home. I grew up with a father who treated me differently from my brothers and I didn't understand why no one else in the family put a stop to it."

Scarlett drew tiny hearts over his chest.

"At least there's a reason I never felt like I belonged in this family."

"Your father's gone," she said. "It's different now."

"Is it? I'm still hovering at the edges of their lives."

She sat up in bed next to him and gathered the sheet around her.

"This cabin is a perfect example," he said. "It sits on the other side of the ranch away from the main house. I'm part of the family, but they don't want me too close."

"Are you sure it's them and not *you* choosing to keep your distance?"

Scarlett's question reverberated inside Reid's head. He sat up next to her and pondered the idea that maybe he was *choosing* not to get close to his family. He'd intentionally picked a career path that had led him away from Stampede and his family. He'd made no effort to visit them through the years. And it was only because of Jessie that he'd come back now. It wasn't fair to blame his family, when he'd made up the rules of the game.

"You can't change the past, Reid, but you can decide the future."

A burning pain squeezed his chest. "You make it sound simple."

"If anyone understands families aren't *simple*, it's me."

He kissed her forehead. "You're a special woman, Scarlett Johnson."

"Families are made up of imperfect people. When you become frustrated with your grandfather or brothers, remind yourself that there's more at stake than just your feelings. Your family is now Jessie's family."

It wouldn't be fair to take his daughter away from her relatives. And he for sure didn't want Jessie to feel like an outcast in her own family—he wouldn't wish that on any person. "Your boss should give you a raise."

"I wasn't offering advice as Jessie's social worker." She gazed into his eyes. "I care about you, Reid." She placed her hand over his heart. "And I'm part of the Hardell family now, too. We're all in this together."

He trapped her fingers against his chest. "But that's just it, Scarlett. I'm not really a Hardell."

"Different genes won't erase your relationships with your grandfather or brothers."

Reid kissed her—he couldn't get enough of her lips. He rolled her beneath him, then froze when he heard pounding on the front door. "It's probably Logan checking on the horse."

Scarlett scrambled off the bed and tugged on her clothes. "No one is to know about this," she whispered.

Reid grinned as he slipped into his jeans.

Scarlett smoothed a hand over her hair and he wanted to tell her not to worry about her appearance because her swollen lips and smudged mascara confirmed they'd been partaking in a little afternoon delight. She escaped the bedroom before Reid finished dressing. He threw on his shirt but left it untucked and walked barefoot into the main room where he came face-to-face with Jessie, not Logan.

His daughter's gaze dropped to his bare feet, then she smiled. "You and Scarlett are boyfriend and girlfriend."

Caught in the act, he didn't have the courage to lie so he didn't say anything.

"I'm glad. I like Scarlett."

"How did you get here?" he asked.

She pointed out the front door. "Grandpa dropped me off."

"Did Scarlett go back to the house with him?"

Jessie nodded, then grabbed the shopping bag Scarlett had left behind. "Did you look at my new quilt?"

"No. Let's see it," he said, happy to change the subject.

"Wait until I put it on my bed." She took the bag into her room and closed the door.

Reid went outside to check on the horse but it was

gone and his truck sat in the drive. A note had been tacked to the porch rail.

"We were worried about you. Gunner rode the horse back to the stable. L."

Great. Now his brothers knew he and Scarlett had slept together, too.

So much for keeping their relationship a secret from the family.

Chapter Ten

Thursday morning Reid sat outside the cabin on the porch steps drinking his morning coffee. He hadn't gotten much sleep lately—par for the course since his world had been rocked in more ways than one the previous Saturday.

Last night he'd stared at the ceiling for hours, trying to make sense of his whole life. He couldn't help thinking that if he'd known the truth about his father, he would have made different choices. But a secret had sent him down the path he'd taken after high school. He'd left Paradise Ranch intending never to return and now here he was, trying to put roots down for Jessie and him in the very place that had never felt like home.

And then there was Scarlett. Sweet, beautiful, caring Scarlett.

He'd never wanted to get married but Jessie and Scarlett had him rethinking that goal. He'd opened up to Scarlett and had shared his vulnerabilities with her— something he'd never done with any other woman. The brief, casual affairs he'd had in the past had left him empty, which had been his intention. If he didn't let people get close to him, he couldn't get hurt. Then Jessie had come into his life and had carved out a piece of his heart.

And then Scarlett had walked into the picture and his heart as if she'd always belonged there. For a man who'd shut himself off from personal relationships he was drowning in them now. Even with all the anxiety and fear he felt at not being the kind of father Jessie deserved or the kind of man Scarlett needed, he couldn't imagine moving forward in life without them.

He and Scarlett hadn't discussed their slip up in his bedroom. And suppers at the main house were hectic, so he hadn't been able to get her alone since they'd made love, but he wasn't worried. This Saturday the whole family, except Lydia and the baby, was going to check out a carnival in Rustler's Creek that was sponsored by A&B Productions. He was hoping to get time alone with Scarlett then.

The cabin door opened and Jessie stepped outside with Fang. The dog scrambled down the steps, then trotted across the yard and peed against the tire of Reid's truck.

Jessie sat next to him. "Why does Fang do that?"

"He's making sure I know he's the boss of you."

Jessie's smiled.

"Hungry?"

She nodded.

"I can try pancakes this morning." So far he'd only made scrambled eggs and made toast for breakfast since she'd begun sleeping at the cabin.

"I know how to make pancakes," she said.

"Then you're in charge of breakfast." He sipped his coffee, keeping an eye on the dog, so the mutt didn't disappear into the woods. "Did you and your mom cook together?"

"No, but when she worked late, I made my own meals."

"Maybe you and I can whip up a few meals and have supper by ourselves at the cabin. We don't always have to go up to the main house for dinner."

Fang trotted back to the porch and crawled into Jessie's lap. She wrapped him in her sweatshirt. "I texted Scarlett last night and told her that I wanted to take a tour of the school."

Reid narrowed is eyes. "How come you didn't tell me?"

"I am telling you."

He looked away, hiding the disappointment and hurt he felt that Jessie hadn't come to him first with the news.

"Scarlett texted me back and said we're supposed to be at the school at ten."

"Today?"

Jessie nodded. "Scarlett's boss, Mrs. Smith, is gonna be there."

Why hadn't Scarlett phoned him? He was the parent. "We better get a move on then." They headed inside.

After breakfast Jessie called first dibs on the shower.

Fortunately she hadn't reached the teenage phase where she spent hours primping in the bathroom. The girl was in and out in twenty minutes.

She walked into the living room in her bathrobe. "What should I wear?"

"You're asking me?"

She nodded.

"I don't know anything about young ladies' clothing."

"Should I wear a dress or jeans and a T-shirt?"

"It's cool today. What about a sweater with a pair of jeans?"

"Okay." She disappeared inside her bedroom.

Reid took his shower and dressed, then sat at his computer and searched job listings until it was time to leave. He couldn't find any auto repair businesses within fifteen miles of Stampede. Maybe he should consider advertising his mechanic services in the classifieds. People could drop their vehicles off at the cabin and he'd work on them in the yard. After a career in the military where he'd been told what to do 24/7 the idea of being his own boss appealed to him.

He checked the time on his phone, then turned off the computer and walked down the hall to tell Jessie they had to leave for the school. He stopped outside her door when he heard her talking on her phone.

"My dad's taking me to the middle school today for a tour. If I decide not to go there, then he's gonna find someone to homeschool me."

Silence.

"Yeah, I like it here. And guess what, Mrs. Delgado? There's a petting zoo at the ranch."

Jessie was talking to her social worker in El Paso.

"Fang likes it, too. My grandpa spoils him and lets him sleep in the dirty clothes basket."

The next sentence out of Jessie's mouth surprised Reid.

"And my dad has a new girlfriend. Her name's Scarlett. She's my aunts' cousin and she's my new social worker."

Reid checked his watch. He hated to have to end Jessie's conversation with Mrs. Delgado, but they needed to leave.

He knocked on the door. "Ready, Jessie?"

"I gotta go," Jessie said. "Okay, I'll let you know what I'm gonna do. Bye." The door opened.

"Is Fang in his carrier?" Reid asked.

Jessie pointed to the corner of the room where the dog slept soundly. Then she twirled in a slow circle. "Is this okay to wear?"

"You look nice." He noticed she'd put her hair in a ponytail.

The drive into Mesquite took twenty minutes and Jessie fidgeted the whole way. "If you don't like the school, you don't have to enroll."

Her chin jutted. "I know."

"Be sure to ask about extracurricular programs," he said.

"I will." She removed a notepad and a pen from her backpack and waved it at him.

"I'll let you ask all the questions." And he kept that promise. Scarlett's boss, Mrs. Smith, was waiting for them in the principal's office when they arrived. Next, they visited with an academic counselor who suggested Jessie take an aptitude test over the summer and depending on her score, she'd be placed in the appropriate classes. After the academic meeting Mrs. Smith left the school and Reid and Jessie were given a tour. He waited in the hallway while Jessie checked out the girls' locker room, then they saw the cafeteria and the music and art rooms before being dropped off at the library.

Reid browsed the bookshelves while Jessie asked the librarian questions about the after-school book club. When the woman showed Jessie how to use the digital book catalogue, his daughter's eyes widened with excitement. After a half hour she thanked the librarian and joined him in the reading nook.

"Anything else you want to check out?" he asked.

"No, I'm good."

During the drive back to the ranch Jessie said, "If I go to school, Fang will be home alone all day."

"Whatever you decide, it'll all work out." He didn't want to get Jessie's hopes up because it might not happen, but if he worked on cars at the cabin, Fang wouldn't be alone.

"I think I want to go to school this fall," she said.

"You don't have to make a decision right away."

"I know, but the library is so cool, and they have a girls' book club that meets once a week."

"You'd probably make some nice friends in that club," he said.

The rest of the drive Jessie chatted about the school and how cool it was that she could download books from the library to her Kindle.

The more she talked, the more animated and confident she grew. Now that Jessie had chosen public school over homeschooling the door had closed on any last thoughts of leaving the ranch. No more dragging his feet.

Reid had to forgive and move on.

"Do you think Fang will be okay all by himself today?" Jessie asked Saturday morning when Reid pulled up to the ranch house.

"Fang will be fine. You gave him plenty of food and fresh water. And we left the light on over the kitchen sink, so he won't be in the dark if it's late by the time we return."

"What if he pees on something?"

Reid had thought about that, too, but he didn't have the heart to lock the dog in the carrier all day while they were gone. "Then we'll clean up the mess."

He parked next to Gunner's pickup—his brother was sitting behind the wheel talking on his phone. The front door opened and Logan escorted the twins to the van and Sadie followed them. Emmett and Amelia got into Gunner's pickup.

"Where's Aunt Lydia and the baby?"

"They're staying home today."

Finally Scarlett came out of the house and surprised Reid when she walked over to his vehicle. He lowered the passenger-side window. "Mind if I ride along with you two?" she asked.

"I'll get in the back." Jessie opened the door.

"You don't have to," Scarlett said, but Jessie ignored her.

"Good morning." He smiled, thinking Scarlett looked like a college coed in her blue jeans and UW Madison sweatshirt. Once they'd buckled up, Reid followed Logan's van and Gunner brought up the rear.

"So why are we going to this carnival anyway?" Jessie asked.

"It's run by the same entertainment company that Amelia booked for the Stampede Rodeo and Spring Festival."

"Why does Stampede have a festival?"

Scarlett shifted in her seat and looked over her shoulder. "It's an excuse to make money for the town and to celebrate the coming of spring."

"Does Grandpa hate spring? Is that why he doesn't want Aunt Amelia to do the rodeo?"

"Gramps doesn't hate spring," Reid said. "He just enjoys sparring with Amelia."

"What's sparring?"

"Arguing," Scarlett said.

Reid flipped on the blinker and merged onto the highway. Scarlett was unusually quiet and he worried that she'd tagged along with them not because she'd missed him, but because she wanted to observe his and Jessie's relationship.

"Hey, Jessie," Reid said. "Have you ever played organized sports?"

"No. Did you?" Jessie asked.

"Baseball," he said.

"Were you good?" Jessie asked.

"I had a decent arm."

"What's that mean?" Jessie asked.

"I could throw a baseball pretty far. Our team played in the state finals my senior year, but we lost." He remembered the awkward moment after the game when all the parents had posed for pictures with their kids and he'd had to stand off to the side by himself because neither of his parents had come. His grandfather and brothers had made it to a few games earlier in the season but Gramps had stayed home to watch over the ranch during the championships because his father had been rodeoing.

"Do girls play baseball?"

"They usually play softball, but yeah, girls play baseball, too."

"Can I play softball?"

"Sure." Reid had never pictured himself involved in youth sports, but it might be fun to coach a girls' softball team. "I can teach you how to throw," he said. "I bet my old baseball glove is still in the attic."

"You could show Tommy and Tyler how to throw a baseball, too."

"Yes, I could." Jessie's suggestion reminded Reid that he hadn't spent any time with his nephews since he'd arrived in town. Jessie had taken a huge leap of faith when she'd decided to attend public school in the fall and it was his turn to leap. If he made more of an effort to be a part of his family, maybe the ranch would become the home it should have been when he'd grown up here. And if he needed more motivation than that, then all he had to do was lock gazes with the woman sitting next to him to know that he didn't want to leave her behind.

"What carnival ride is your favorite?" Scarlett asked Jessie when Reid turned into the fairground parking lot.

"The Scrambler." Jessie unbuckled her belt. "Mom took me to a carnival when I was in third grade and she squished me on the ride."

Reid stopped the pickup when they reached the lot attendant. He lowered the window and handed him a ten-dollar bill. Gunner and Logan were directed to park one aisle over. The familiar scent of greasy fry bread, corn dogs and popcorn greeted his nose when he got out of the truck. Not until they reached the entrance did Reid catch a whiff of the animal barns.

He paid their admission fee, waving off Scarlett's attempt to cover her own ticket. After they walked through the gate, they stepped aside and waited for the rest of the family.

"Emmett and I are going off on our own," Amelia announced. "I have a list of things I want to check on."

"My dogs are gonna bark after following you all over hell's half acre," Gramps said.

Gunner grinned. "I'll chaperone the love birds."

"The boys want to go on the kiddie rides," Sadie said. "Logan and I will be over there." She pointed to an inflatable arch with *Kiddie Land* spelled across it.

The group split up, leaving Reid, Jessie and Scarlett at the entrance. "I guess you two are stuck with me," Scarlett said.

Reid couldn't think of anyone else he'd rather be "stuck" with than Scarlett.

Jessie tugged Scarlett's hand. "Let's go on the Scrambler."

"Hey, I like the ride, too." Reid grabbed Scarlett's other hand, his spirits lifting when her fingers gripped his tighter.

Jessie led the way to the ticket booth, where Reid purchased a handful of tickets, then they got in line for the ride. After a ten-minute wait the operator opened the gate and they climbed into one of the compartments.

"Scarlett can sit in the middle," Jessie said. "I don't want to get smashed."

Reid got in first, followed by Scarlett and Jessie. The operator checked the safety bar on the compartments, then returned to his station and the ride began moving. As it picked up speed, Jessie's squeals grew louder and Scarlett's body pushed harder against Reid—the ride's speed, her laughter and the smell of her perfume making him light-headed. Eventually the ride slowed to a stop. After the attendant released the safety latch, they staggered to the exit.

"Let's do the fun house!" Jessie snagged Scarlett's arm and pulled her through the crowd to Bob's Big

House of Fun. Reid chuckled at his daughter's excitement, happy she was enjoying herself.

The operator collected their tickets. "Watch the moving floors."

"Me first." Jessie walked carefully across the swaying bridge. As soon as she reached the other end, she descended three jiggling steps and disappeared.

Scarlett started across the bridge but teetered after a few seconds and Reid wrapped an arm around her waist. "I've got you." He wished he could hold her longer, but Jessie's voice rang out.

"Are you guys coming?"

"We're almost there!" Scarlett navigated the remaining three feet of walkway and then she and Reid joined Jessie in the hall of mirrors. Scarlett and Jessie laughed and giggled at their three-foot-tall reflections, and Reid easily pictured the three of them doing more things together in the future.

"We look like Oompa Loompas," Scarlett said.

"What's an Oompa Loompa?" Jessie asked.

Scarlett gasped. "You've never seen the movie *Charlie and the Chocolate Factory*?"

Jessie shook her head and Scarlett looked at Reid.

He shrugged. "Neither have I."

"We'll have to watch the movie sometime." She took Jessie's hand and they zigzagged through the crooked hallway before arriving at the barrel roll. Jessie hopped inside first as the cylinder turned. Gravity knocked her to her knees then, laughing, she crawled out the other side. "I'll wait for you guys at the end."

"Let's do this together." Reid took Scarlett's hand.

She smiled. "You better not fall on me."

He pulled her against his side. "How about you fall on me."

Her brown eyes darkened. "You're not supposed to look at me like that."

"You mean—" his head inched closer "—like I want to kiss you?"

She nodded, her gaze fixated on his mouth.

"I'm going to kiss you." He nuzzled her neck.

"I'm Jessie's social worker."

"I know."

She curled into him. "I'm serious, Reid."

"I can tell you're serious." He kissed her—a short but deep kiss that lasted a few seconds. "Is that why you've been avoiding me this week? Because you know you can't resist me?"

"You're such a smart man." Children's laughter echoed behind them. "I'll bet you a corn dog that you fall first."

"Forget the corn dog," he said, "I want another kiss." They stepped in the barrel and managed to remain upright until Reid saw Scarlett lick her lips, then he forgot to move his legs and his size thirteen feet tripped over themselves. He dropped like a felled tree.

Scarlett laughed when he struggled to stand. "You think that's funny?" he asked.

"I want mustard on my corn dog."

He caressed her inner thigh and she lost her balance, her arms windmilling. Reid caught her as she fell, making sure she landed on top of him. They lay at the bottom of the moving barrel, her breasts pressing into his chest, her breath puffing against his chin. Their gazes locked.

He slid his fingers into her hair and gave her a quick

kiss that he hoped conveyed how much he wished they were tumbling in a bed and not a barrel. Then he helped her to her feet and they climbed out.

Scarlett caught his arm before they went any further. "Lipstick." She rubbed her thumb over the corner of his mouth. Her smile faded and her brown eyes grew serious. "No more. Promise?"

He grinned. "I'll think about it."

When they reached the exit, Jessie asked, "Can you win me a giant bear?" She pointed to Game Alley where humungous stuffed animals hung inside the booths.

"It's been a while since I've thrown a baseball, but I'm willing to give it a try." They stopped at the milk bottle toss and he said, "You know these games are rigged, don't you?"

"How?" Jessie asked.

"If you weigh the milk cans, the two at the bottom will be heavier than the one on top and—" he pointed to the bottom can on the right "—that one is sticking out a half inch farther from the other one. It'll absorb the impact and remain upright."

Jessie glanced between the giant stuffed bears hanging inside the tent and Reid. "You said you were good at baseball."

Scarlett elbowed him. "You'll just have to throw the ball really hard."

"Lucky me," he said. "I got stuck with the sassy ladies today." He approached the game operator. "Six balls, please." He picked up the first one and looked over his shoulder at his audience. "And they fill these with cork so they're lighter than a normal softball."

"Excuses, excuses," Scarlett said.

Reid wound up his arm but stopped short of throwing the ball when he heard someone call his name.

"Uncle Reid!" Tommy and Tyler sprinted toward him while Logan and Sadie hurried to catch up.

"Are you gonna win Jessie one of those?" Tyler pointed to a prize.

"I hope so," Reid said.

"I want the white bear," Jessie said, then looked at the twins. "He'll win you guys a bear, too." Her gaze swung to Reid. "Right, Dad?"

Reid's heart stopped beating inside his chest. He'd been waiting for this moment since the day he and Jessie had been introduced to each other. He doubted she even realized she'd called him *Dad* but the one-syllable word turned his heart into a puddle of mush.

He thought he'd been prepared for this moment but his childhood flashed before his eyes. He'd stopped calling Donny Hardell *Dad* when he'd entered the third grade. Even as a young kid, Reid had known fathers weren't supposed to treat their children like dirt. He was humbled that Jessie had gifted him her trust and he'd do everything in his power to make sure she'd never regret calling him *Dad*.

"Uncle Reid." Tommy tugged on Reid's pant leg. "Will you win a bear for me?"

"Me, too," Tyler said.

Logan chuckled. "C'mon, Mr. Baseball. Show us what you've got."

After Jessie called him *Dad*, Reid felt like he could do anything. "Stand back and be amazed." The first ball knocked over the top can and pushed the bottom two cans farther apart. After two more throws, one can was left standing. "That was my practice round." Reid handed the operator a twenty. "This time," he whispered, "Stand the bottom cans next to each other."

The operator glanced at the twins and then nodded. Now Reid had a chance to win and impress his nephews and daughter. And Scarlett. But when he turned, she was gone. She'd walked several yards away to take a phone call and stood with her back to him.

"I bet ten dollars you can't knock them all over." Logan waved the bill in front of Reid's face.

"You're on." Reid made a big production of winding up his arm. He checked over his shoulder once to see if Scarlett was watching but she was still on the phone. The boys cheered louder and he let the first softball fly. *Bingo!* All three cans toppled.

"You did it, Dad! You did it!" Jessie clapped.

"Pick out your bear." Reid took the money his brother had lost and gave it to the game operator. "Keep that for yourself." The man lined up the cans evenly again and Reid knocked them all over with his second throw. He nodded to the twins. "One of you pick a prize."

Tommy pushed his brother forward. "You first, Tyler." The boy asked for the brown bear.

Reid nodded to the operator. "One more time and then we'll move on." The man blew out a breath and nodded, obviously grateful he wouldn't be losing more than three prizes to the group. Reid glanced at Scarlett again and tamped down his disappointment that she was still on the phone and not watching him. He wondered what was so important that she couldn't speak to the person after they left the carnival.

Reid played up the dramatics again and then threw the ball, toppling the cans for a third time. The operator handed Tommy a black bear. Both boys hugged one of Reid's legs and shouted, "Thank you, Uncle Reid!"

Jessie squeezed his waist. "Thanks, Dad."

Logan walked over and slapped Reid on the back. "I knew you'd come through for the kids."

For the first time since he'd been home, Reid felt a bond with his older brother.

Chapter Eleven

"Come in." Scarlett glanced over her shoulder and saw Sadie enter the bedroom. As soon as her cousin noticed the suitcase on the bed, she closed the door.

"What are you doing?"

Scarlett was so angry and upset with herself that she had to take a deep breath before answering. "I'm packing."

"I can see that." Sadie sat on the end of the bed. "What's going on?"

"This isn't a good time, Sadie." She squeezed her eyes closed to keep the tears from falling.

"Did you and Reid have an argument?"

"Why would you think that?"

"Maybe because you rode home from the carnival in our van and not with Reid and Jessie."

She opened the dresser drawer and emptied the contents into the suitcase. "I can't talk about this now."

Sadie snapped her fingers. "Does this have something to do with the phone call you took at the carnival?" When Scarlett didn't answer, her cousin grabbed her arm. "We've always been able to talk about anything."

Maybe if she let the cat out of the bag, she'd finally

be able to take a deep breath. "I was speaking with my supervisor on the phone."

"Did something happen to one of the kids in your care?"

"Lois asked me to come into her office first thing Monday morning."

"Did she say why?"

"No," Scarlett lied. Her boss had told her exactly why she needed to speak to Scarlett.

"It's probably nothing." Sadie nodded to the luggage. "Where are you going?"

"I'm moving in with Aunt Amelia. Tomorrow I'm looking for an apartment in Mesquite." She should have gotten her own place as soon as she'd moved to Texas, but she'd let her cousin convince her to stay at the house so she could be closer to the family.

Don't blame Sadie. This isn't her fault.

"It's kind of late to be going to Aunt Amelia's. She and Emmett are probably in bed."

Scarlett ignored the comment. "I'm sure Emmett will be glad to get his bedroom here at the house back. All he does is complain about Aunt Amelia."

"I doubt it."

"He can stay or go. I don't care," Scarlett said. There were plenty of bedrooms in her aunt's Victorian. Scarlett zipped the suitcase, then set it on the floor and shrugged into her coat.

"Are you sure there's nothing I can do to help?"

Scarlett squeezed Sadie's hands. "I'm fine. Enjoy having your house back to yourself."

"I'll call Aunt Amelia and tell her you're on the way," Sadie said.

"Don't." Scarlett winced when she spoke louder than

she'd meant to. She smiled even though she felt sick to her stomach. "If you want, you can come with me tomorrow to look at apartments. I'll call you when I get up in the morning."

Scarlett grabbed her purse, then carried her suitcase down the stairs and out the front door. When she glanced in the rearview mirror as she drove away, she spotted Sadie standing on the porch. The first tear fell and by the time she reached the main road, she was sobbing. She parked the car, then sat and cried until all her tears were spent, then she wiped her eyes, blew her nose and drove into town.

When she arrived at the old Victorian, Emmett's pickup blocked the driveway so she left her car on the street. She wheeled her suitcase up the sidewalk, noticing the second-floor lights were on but the first story was dark. Scarlett rang the bell and waited. When a full minute passed, she pressed the bell again, wondering if her aunt was in the shower and Emmett had already fallen asleep.

The door opened and her aunt stood in the foyer dressed in a silky pink nightgown and matching bathrobe. "Scarlett?"

"Aunt Amelia." She made a weak attempt to smile. "I'm sorry to disturb you, but I need a place to stay."

Her aunt's gaze shifted to the suitcase, then she waved Scarlett inside. "What happened?"

"It's a long story."

"Amelia, I'm ready!" Emmett's voice echoed from the second floor.

"I'll be right there, dear." Amelia smiled and then whispered, "He doesn't understand that those little blue pills last longer than ten minutes."

Scarlett didn't know what to say, mostly because she'd never pictured her aunt and Reid's grandfather in bed together at their age. "Never mind, Aunt Amelia. I can see I came at a bad time."

Her aunt grasped her arm. "You're not leaving. This only takes five minutes. Make yourself at home." Her aunt climbed the stairs, her pink robe floating in the air behind her.

Scarlett left the suitcase in the foyer and slipped outside to wait on the porch. Maybe the cool air would clear her head. She sat in the rocker and drew her legs up to her chest, then rested her chin on her knees. Her boss's words echoing through her head…

Please come into my office as soon as you arrive at work. I need to discuss a possible breach of the National Association of Social Workers code of ethics.

Her supervisor had refused to go into detail over the phone but told Scarlett she was to have no contact with Jessie or her father. No texting. No phone calls. Nothing until Lois said otherwise.

All Scarlett could think of was that one of her co-workers had been at the carnival and had seen Reid and her holding hands and then had called Lois. She rubbed her forehead, trying to push her supervisor's words out of her mind.

Scarlett could kick herself for being so careless. If Lois asked about her living arrangements on Monday, she wanted to be able to say that she had her own apartment and no longer lived at the ranch. After what had happened with Dale, she couldn't believe she'd allowed herself to get caught in this position again—falling for the father of one of her clients. All she ever wanted to do was help kids, but she kept screwing up.

The front door opened and Aunt Amelia stepped outside, wearing a winter robe and slippers. She handed Scarlett a mug. "Green tea. You can never have enough antioxidants." She sat in the other rocking chair. "Are you coming down with a cold? Your eyes look swollen."

"I didn't mean to interrupt your romantic evening."

Her aunt flashed an impish smiled. "Our romantic evenings come to an end after Emmett has his way with me, then passes out and sleeps like a baby all night."

"How long have you been in love with Emmett, Aunt Amelia?"

"Since high school. He never thought he was good enough for me. And my stupid ploy to make him jealous by dating your uncle backfired when I got pregnant." Amelia pursed her lips and stared across the street. "I don't know why your uncle and I stayed married after I miscarried. I guess it just worked out because he traveled all the time. He did his thing and I did mine." She squeezed Scarlett's hand. "I'm the one who convinced Emmett to marry Sara. Before she died, she told me that she'd always known I was in love with Emmett all those years. She gave me her blessing to be with him."

"That was a long time ago."

"Emmett's a stubborn fool. He won't let himself be with me because he's punishing himself."

"For what?"

"For letting me get away."

Scarlett wiggled her eyebrows. "Was it worth the wait?"

Amelia laughed. "It was indeed."

"Why haven't you two married?"

"He won't propose to me."

"Maybe you should do the asking."

Her aunt nodded. "I'll take your suggestion under consideration."

"What's the worst that can happen?" Scarlett asked.

"He'll say no and we'll keep doing what we're doing."

"Which is?"

"Chasing each other in circles like a pair of rabid dogs."

Scarlett laughed.

"Enough about my love life," Aunt Amelia said. "Why did you show up on my doorstep this late at night?"

"I can't say anything about it just yet."

"You can always talk to me in confidence, dear."

"I know." Scarlett sipped her tea. "I won't overstay my welcome. Tomorrow I'm searching for an apartment."

"Emmett's sleeping in the room the twins used when Sadie stayed here. The bed in the yellow room has fresh linens on it."

"Thank you."

"You make yourself at home, dear."

"I appreciate that." But the sooner she moved out the better. No way did she want to hear Emmett and her aunt carrying on in the bedroom down the hall. Scarlett followed her aunt inside and they parted ways on the second-floor landing.

A half hour later, she crawled into the queen-size canopy bed in the yellow room and snuggled beneath the covers. Her last thought before she drifted off to sleep was that maybe she'd picked the wrong profession.

"WHERE IS EVERYONE?" Reid asked his grandfather early Sunday afternoon when he stepped into the kitchen at the main house.

"Logan's out at the stables with the twins taking care of the horses. Gunner's watching the baby and I'm trying to figure out what to make for supper."

"Where are Scarlett, Lydia and Sadie?"

"They drove into Mesquite to check out an apartment complex Scarlett's thinking about moving into."

Why hadn't Scarlett told him she was looking for an apartment? She'd had plenty of time at the carnival to bring it up. His grandfather set a mug of coffee on the table. "Did she say when she plans to move out?"

His grandfather frowned. "Thought you knew."

"Knew what?"

"Scarlett packed her bags and spent last night in the guest bedroom at Amelia's house."

Reid studied the dark brew inside his cup. Scarlett didn't drive home from the carnival with him and Jessie yesterday and then she moved out of the house last night. Something was going on and he didn't like being in the dark. He'd text her when he had privacy and ask her to call him ASAP. "Don't tell Sadie I said this, but your coffee is better than hers."

The old man chuckled. "Your grandmother was jealous of my talents in the kitchen."

"Who taught you?"

"My mother."

"Did my mom ever take us kids to see her parents in Oklahoma?"

"She took you up once before Gunner came along."

"Me and Logan?"

"Only you."

"Why just me?" Logan asked.

"Donny thought your mom was going to meet with your biological father. He wouldn't let Logan go because he was afraid your mama might decide to stay in Oklahoma for good."

"But she came back."

Gramps nodded.

"Why didn't Mom take us kids with her when she finally left the ranch for good?"

"She knew Donny would make her life miserable so she cut ties with all of us."

Reid hadn't been that close to his mother and he hadn't cried when she'd left, but Gunner had and Reid remembered feeling sorry for his younger brother.

"How's the job search going?" Gramps asked.

"About that," Reid said. "I noticed that there aren't any car-repair businesses around Stampede. Do you think if I fixed cars at the cabin I could drum up enough business?"

"If you opened a shop in Stampede you might."

"I don't have the capital to buy a piece of property."

Gramps grinned. "I happen to know a wealthy woman who's looking to invest in the town."

"You think Amelia would give me a low-interest loan?"

"She'd probably hand over the money for free, if you bought the old Amoco station and fixed it up."

Reid fetched the coffeepot and topped off their mugs. "You wouldn't mind putting in a good word with Amelia for me?"

"Be happy to. The busier I can keep that woman the less she nags me."

"You like her pushing and prodding you."

"I'm retired. I'm supposed to sit on my keister all day and do nothing, if I want."

Reid hid a smile behind his mug. They both knew

Emmett's bluster was all bark and no bite. "Thanks for the coffee. I'm heading back to the cabin to pick up Jessie."

"What are you two up to?"

"I told her I'd take her on another horseback ride."

"Supper's at five thirty tonight."

"We'll be there." In fact he'd be early, because he intended to find out what was going on with Scarlett. Reid took his mug to the sink, then left the house. When he pulled up to the cabin Jessie and Fang were lounging on the steps along with Stacy's cremation urn. He got out of the pickup and walked over to the porch.

"Looks like you've got something on your mind," he said.

"Instead of horseback riding will you show me the place Grandpa put your grandma's ashes?"

"You sure you're ready?" When Jessie moved into the cabin, she'd put the urn on the dresser in her bedroom.

"I want my mom to be part of our family, too, even though she's not here. And I can visit her whenever I want."

Reid was proud of his daughter. She was a tough little girl. "Okay, then. Let's go." They climbed into the truck and he drove along a dirt road through the woods for a half mile before leaving the path and driving a short ways across the bumpy ground. Then he stopped and turned off the engine.

"This is it?" Jessie asked, staring out the windshield.

"We have to walk the rest of the way. A quarter mile over there—" he pointed out the windshield "—is the stream and nearby is my grandmother's wildflower garden."

Jessie put the leash on Fang and they began their trek. After a few minutes Jessie asked, "Are you and Scarlett gonna get married?"

"I like Scarlett a lot, but it's too soon to talk about marriage."

"Why?"

"Relationships take time to grow."

"You didn't know my mom but you had sex with her right away."

Reid felt like a cornered animal and wished Scarlett were here to help him navigate the conversation. "I'm older and wiser now than when I met your mother. Relationships that last are ones built on love and respect, not just sex."

"Do you regret what you did with my mom?"

"I regret that I wasn't there to help your mother raise you." He tugged on Jessie's ponytail. "Your mom was brave and strong and I admire her for taking good care of you all by herself. I'll always be grateful to her for loving you and keeping you safe."

Jessie stopped walking. "I think Mom would be happy that Stampede is our forever home."

"I think she would, too." No matter how far Reid had tried to run from his family, Paradise Ranch would always be home. If anyone hadn't belonged here it had been Donny Hardell—not Reid. When they continued walking, he said, "I might have an idea for what to do with Fang once school starts in the fall."

"What?"

"I'm looking into opening my own business in town."

"What kind of business?"

"A mechanics garage. If I do, Fang could come to work with me every day."

Jessie's face lit up. "Really?"

"Nothing's for sure. I'm going to call the bank tomorrow and make an appointment to speak with a loan officer." It was risky letting Jessie get her hopes up, but not wanting to disappoint her would motivate him to find a way to make this happen.

They continued along the path until the stream came into view. "See those flowers over there?" He pointed to the black-eyed Susans. "That's where my grandmother and father's ashes are spread." When they reached the flowerbed, Reid hung back and gave Jessie some privacy.

"Can we get one of those for my mom?" She pointed to the heart-shaped memorial stones on the ground.

"Of course." He cleared his throat. "Would you like to say something before you spread her ashes?"

Jessie dropped to her knees and Reid watched her lips move, but he couldn't make out the whispered words. Then she stood and looked over her shoulder. "How do I do this?"

He moved closer. "There's no right or wrong way. You can sprinkle the ashes over the whole area or put them all in one spot."

Jessie's eyes flicked between the urn, the wildflowers and the sky. She moved a few feet to her right. "Mom can see the sun better from here." She removed the lid and handed it to Reid. Then she slowly poured the ashes in one spot before placing her hand on top of the mound. When she stood she faced the sun and blew the dust off her palm.

A sudden gust of wind lifted Jessie's ponytail in the air and she said, "I think my mom likes this place."

Reid's eyes burned, but he managed a smile for his daughter.

Jessie brushed her hands against her jeans, leaving a smudge of ash dust on the denim. When she turned away from the flowers, he held out his arms and Jessie walked into them. They hugged for a long time and in that moment Reid made a silent vow to Stacy that he'd always be there for their little girl. He carried the empty urn back to the truck and waited while Jessie gave Fang a few minutes to sniff the ground along the stream bank.

"We still have time for a horseback ride?" Jessie asked when she climbed into the pickup.

"A short one." He drove out to the stables, where they found Logan grooming one of the horses. Tommy was helping him and Tyler was reading in the back of Logan's truck.

As soon as the boys saw Jessie they raced toward her. "JJ's here!" Tommy yelled.

Jessie went into the barn with the boys and they played on the hay bales. Reid walked over to Logan. "Would it be all right if Jessie and I went riding?"

"Sure." Logan eyed Reid, then said, "Gramps told me you're thinking about buying the old gas station in town and turning it into an auto repair shop."

Jeez. "He must have called you as soon as I left the house a little while ago."

Logan grinned.

"I plan to talk with Amelia at supper tonight and see if she'll cosign a bank loan for me. I still have to figure out where I'm going to get the money for the down payment."

"I might have an idea."

"I'm listening."

"You could borrow the money you've been sending home all these years. There's almost forty thousand in that savings account."

Reid admired the hell out of his brother. Logan could have easily used that cash to save his own skin when he'd fallen behind on the mortgage payments. Instead, he'd accepted responsibility for his mistakes and had allowed Amelia to turn Paradise Ranch into a tourist attraction in exchange for her covering the missed mortgage payments.

"Stampede is a small town. It'll be risky making a go of it. I'm not sure the bank will be supportive even if Amelia is backing the loan."

"Gunner's gotten really good at that social media stuff," Logan said. "He could design a website for the business and help you advertise it."

"It's still a gamble." There was more on the line than money. "Jessie really likes the school in Mesquite and wants to enroll this fall."

"It sounds like you're set on staying then."

Reid nodded. "If you and Gunner don't mind."

"Mind? We've been waiting for you to come back for years. Paradise Ranch is as much your home as it is ours, Reid. You and Jessie could remodel the cabin if you need more space."

"Jessie would like that."

"What about you?" Logan asked.

Maybe it was time to admit that he wanted a do-over with his brothers. "I think I'd like to stay, too."

Chapter Twelve

"Don't hate me." Eileen set a new folder on top of the mountain of paperwork on the desk.

Scarlett had come into work a half hour early, hoping she'd be alone in the office. She should have anticipated a handful of coworkers would be trying to get a jumpstart on their to-do lists because there were never enough hours in the day to get all their work done. Getting ahead wasn't a reality in this job—social workers were just happy if they managed to tread water and stay afloat.

Scarlett opened the file. "What's going on with—" she read the name "—Crystal Juarez?"

"Low-needs case that came in late Friday and you were next on the list for new clients."

Kids rotated into the system faster than they rotated out.

Eileen nodded to the folder. "Crystal's foster parents are asking for her to be tested."

"Tested for what?"

Eileen wiggled her fingers and made air quotes. "Issues."

Most kids in the system had issues but that didn't mean they all required testing. "I'll call the parents and speak with them." She glanced at the wall clock above her cubicle. Her boss would be in any minute.

"Oh," Eileen said. "I almost forgot to tell you that Lois isn't coming in until later this afternoon."

"Did she say why?"

"Some kind of emergency. She asked me to tell you to stay put until she gets here." Eileen frowned. "Is everything okay?"

"Sure," Scarlett said. "Why wouldn't it be?"

Eileen returned to her desk and Scarlett made a note on her calendar to phone Crystal's foster parents on Thursday. She spent the morning making other calls and checking up on her clients. She worked through lunch, trying to accomplish as many tasks as possible before her boss returned. It was three thirty when a shadow fell across her desk.

"Scarlett, would you please come into my office?"

"Sure." She followed Lois down the hallway, ignoring the curious glances from her coworkers.

"Shut the door," Lois said. "And sit down."

Lois Smith was an intimidating woman on her best days. On her worst days she was downright terrifying. The forty-five-year-old was built like a tank—sturdy and strong. Her dark beady eyes pinned Scarlett. "I received a troubling call on Saturday."

"From who?"

Lois sat behind her desk and reached for a pen, then pointed the tip at Scarlett. "I can't divulge their name. But I need to know if you and Jessie Jones's father are in a personal relationship."

Scarlett's stomach sank. "When you assigned Jessie's case to me I told you that my cousins are married to Reid—Mr. Hardell's brothers."

"You know what I'm asking, Scarlett."

"I'll be moving into an apartment in Mesquite in two weeks. Until then I'm staying at my aunt's house in Stampede."

"You still haven't answered the question. Are you or aren't you involved with Reid Hardell?"

There was nothing she could say in her defense. "I am."

Lois rubbed her brow. "Because I received this complaint, I contacted your previous supervisor in Madison."

The blood drained from Scarlett's face.

Lois shook her head. "I have no choice but to fire you, Scarlett. I can't have my staff behaving in a way that opens us up to lawsuits."

Scarlett was guilty and she had no right to ask but she did anyway. "You won't consider a suspension without pay?"

"Not for a second offense. After you clean out your personal items, leave your case files, company cell phone and computer with your password and login on your desk." Lois held out her hand. "I'll take your badge."

Scarlett's throat was so tight she could barely breathe let alone swallow. "I'm sorry," she whispered, then turned to leave.

"Scarlett."

She paused with her hand on the doorknob.

"I'm sorry, too. You're great with the kids and you've done a lot of good since you began working here."

The kind words did little to ease Scarlett's pain. She returned to her desk and five minutes later she walked out of the building with only her purse and coat. Scarlett waited until she got into her car and drove away before she allowed the tears to fall. Fearing she'd cause an accident because she couldn't see well, she pulled into the McDonald's parking lot and sat in the car, bawling her head off.

When the tears stopped she strangled the wheel until sharp pains shot through her fingers. She wished she could blame Reid for getting fired, but this was her fault. Scarlett looked in her rearview mirror and the woman staring back at her was a stranger.

"YOU'RE STRUNG TIGHTER than barbed wire," Logan said Monday afternoon. He slipped between the rails of the corral and walked over to Reid, who sat on the bucking machine.

Reid didn't deny the charge. His gut had been tied in a knot because Scarlett still hadn't returned his calls or texts. It wasn't like her to ignore him or Jessie. When she'd skipped Sunday dinner with the family, he'd asked Amelia if anything was the matter. The old woman had avoided eye contact with him and brushed off his concern, which did nothing to quell his anxiety.

Reid hopped off the mechanical bull. "I wanted to practice for the rodeo because I suck." He decided to try the bucking machine after Jessie left with Sadie to pick the twins up from school and take them to their karate lesson. "I thought you had a group of city slickers scheduled for a trail ride this afternoon."

"They canceled. And I'm glad."

"Why's that?"

"Ever since Amelia got it in her head to resurrect Stampede, I've been busier than ever. Sadie and I haven't had a date night in over a month."

"You're married." Reid grinned. "Isn't every evening date night in your bedroom?"

"Funny," Logan said. "Once a week we'd go somewhere without the boys and Gramps would babysit. But with him staying at Amelia's we haven't had any time alone."

"Jessie and I can watch the twins."

Logan slapped Reid on the back and grinned. "I'm going to take you up on your offer."

"You should. It'll give me a chance to teach the boys how to throw a baseball since you don't know how."

Logan shoved Reid. "You're a real cut-up this afternoon."

"Speaking of Gramps," Reid said. "Don't you think he and Amelia should just elope?"

"We've suggested that." Logan poked a finger in Reid's chest. "You tell him. Maybe he'll listen to you."

Reid had enough problems with his own love life. He didn't want to take on his grandfather's troubles.

"How's Jessie liking the cabin?" Logan asked.

"She loves her room and Fang likes sitting on the back of the sofa and looking out the window."

"What about you?"

"I'm having trouble falling asleep. I forgot how quiet the country can be."

"Where did you live in Albuquerque?"

"I rented a studio apartment near a freeway. I fell asleep to the sounds of sirens and eighteen-wheelers."

"You could have afforded a better place if you hadn't sent money home every month," Logan said.

Reid studied the tips of his boots. "I didn't need anything fancy."

"You never had a lady move in with you?"

Reid shook his head.

"No serious relationships?"

"One that lasted a few months. I met Ellen at a bar and we hit it off."

"What happened?"

"Nosey, aren't you," Reid said.

"You're my brother. I can get up in your business, if I want."

Reid didn't mind the teasing—because that was what brothers did. "I broke things off with Ellen when I found out she had a kid."

Logan's eyes rounded.

Reid shrugged. "I never planned on having kids."

"It must have been a heck of a shock when you learned about Jessie."

"When I met Jessie for the first time and saw that she had my eyes…" Reid pressed his hand to his chest. "I can't imagine not having her in my life."

Logan stared into the distance. "Something's been bothering me."

"What?"

"After finding out the truth about Dad and how he treated you—" he stared at Reid "—I can't figure out why you sent money home every month."

"I told myself it was because I wasn't here to help you and Gunner run the ranch or the motel."

"What do you mean you told yourself?"

You can't let go of the past unless you tell the truth. "I never felt like I was part of this family, but you, Gunner and Gramps were all I had left and—"

"You were afraid to write us off." Logan shoved a hand through his hair. "For what it's worth, I'm sorry I wasn't a better big brother. And I'm really sorry I didn't see what Dad was doing."

Reid nodded. "I believe you."

"We had a hell of a dysfunctional childhood," Logan said. "But we're going to do better for our kids."

Amen to that. A horn blast caught their attention. Gunner pulled into the ranch yard.

"What's got you grinning like a fool?" Logan asked when their baby brother joined them inside the corral.

"Lydia gave me the afternoon off from babysitting." He removed his cowboy hat and slapped it against his thigh. "She caught me waking Amelia up."

"On purpose?" Logan asked.

"I've been trying to teach her to say *Da Da*." Gunner shrugged. "I read that the more you talk to babies the faster they learn to speak."

Logan nudged Reid. "Gunner's got more baby books stashed in the motel office than the town library."

"I don't have any advice to offer on babies," Reid said. "But be careful what you wish for because babies grow into tweens and they never stop talking."

"How are things going with getting permanent custody of Jessie?" Gunner asked.

"Good, I guess. Why?" Reid asked.

"I overheard Lydia chatting with Amelia on the phone and your name came up."

"What else did you hear?" Reid asked.

"Nothing. Lydia went into the bedroom and shut the door."

Now Reid wondered if Scarlett hadn't been in touch with him because something had happened with Jessie's case. "Maybe she's working on a court date for the custody hearing." And Reid told himself that if she was she probably didn't want to get his hopes up until she knew for sure and that's why she was keeping her distance from him and Jessie.

"Was Logan giving you pointers?" Gunner nodded to the mechanical bull.

"I was about to," Logan said.

"Good thing I showed up when I did." Gunner puffed out his chest. "You'll want to take my advice."

"Remind me again how many buckles you've won?" Logan asked.

Gunner ignored the barb and spoke to Reid. "Keep your hips forward."

"No, keep your hips still and pull your shoulders back," Logan said.

Reid climbed onto the machine and found out that no matter which brother he listened to the end result was the same—he got tossed after a few seconds.

"Time for a professional to show you how it's done." Logan climbed on but before Gunner flipped the switch, Sadie's van pulled up to the house. A few seconds later Gramps and Fang came out the back door to greet the kids. Instead of going inside, the gang walked over to the corral. The kids climbed the rails and sat on the top rung while Fang rolled on the ground in the dirt.

"Whatcha doing, Dad?" Tommy asked Logan.

"Showing Uncle Reid how to be a cowboy."

Sadie shielded her eyes from the sun. "Who managed to stay on the longest?"

"Me." Logan hopped off the machine, walked over to his wife and gave her a kiss. The twins groaned and Jessie laughed.

"Watch this, boys." Logan walked back to the machine. "Your dad's going to show you how a champion rides."

Reid took the control box out of Gunner's hand. "I've got this." Logan signaled he was ready, so Reid moved the switch to Low and gave his brother a minute to preen in front of the twins.

"Turn it up a notch," Logan shouted.

"How about three notches," Reid whispered.

Gunner chuckled. "Now you're talking, brother."

Reid pushed the toggle upward and the machine jerked right, then left as the front tilted forward. The action repeated in quick succession and Logan's hat flew off his head. Then he slid sideways, struggling to pull himself upright.

"Slow it down some," Gunner said.

Reid did and Logan regained his balance, but not for long. Reid moved the toggle all the way up and Logan went flying. He fell onto the mattress, then scrambled to his feet. "You think that's funny?"

"Uh-oh," Gunner said. "Now we've riled him."

"You said you were the best." Reid glanced at the kids, who gaped at the brothers. Even Sadie and Gramps looked nervous. Reid handed the control box to Gunner and nonchalantly moved closer to the stock tank. Logan stalked him, shoving a finger in his face. "You did that on purpose."

"You sound like a whiny kid." Gunner laughed when Logan stamped his cowboy boot in the dirt.

Quick as lightning Reid grabbed his brother's legs and lifted him into the air, then tossed him over the edge of the tank. Logan hit the water with a big splash.

Reid caught the twins' horrified expressions and

said, "Watch your eyeballs, boys. They're gonna fall out and bounce across the ground."

Jessie gave him a thumbs-up and Reid grinned, unaware Logan was going to make him pay for the stunt until he felt his brother's hands grab the waistband of his jeans and yank him off his feet. Before he had a chance to hold his breath, he hit the water and went under. Reid came up sputtering and coughing to the sound of Logan's gleeful chuckle.

"Someone needed to put you in your place," Logan said.

Gunner wandered closer. "You two ought to just stay in the tank and let me show the kids how a real rodeo cowboy rides."

Reid raised his eyebrow and looked at Logan. His brother nodded and they jumped forward, each grabbing one of Gunner's arms. Their brother dug his heels in but couldn't get away and they yanked him into the water. Jessie jumped to the ground and raced over, the twins hot on her heels. When she reached the tank she splashed Reid.

Logan grabbed Tommy by the waistband of his pants and Gunner did the same to Tyler. The brothers twirled the boys in a circle above their heads and then dropped the squealing kids into the water.

Reid grinned at Jessie when she took a step back. "You think you're too old to have fun?" He grabbed the back of her sweatshirt when she turned to run. A moment later he'd lifted her high and dropped her into the water.

Jessie broke the surface, laughing and coughing as she peeled her long hair away from her eyes. A splash war kicked off and within a few minutes they'd created a mud bog in the corral. Fang barked at the commotion and twirled in circles. Reid caught their grandfather grinning from ear to ear and Sadie taping the commotion on her iPhone.

After a few minutes Sadie insisted they get out of the water before they caught colds. She went into the house and returned with a handful of towels, which she placed over the corral rail.

"Bring them closer," Logan said.

Sadie laughed. "Not on your life. I'll be inside."

Reid helped Jessie out of the tank but as soon as her shoes hit the muddy ground her feet slid out from under her and she landed on her rump, splashing mud in her face. "You okay?" Reid climbed out and offered her a hand up. Instead of getting to her feet, she yanked him forward and his boots slid in separate directions. He lost his balance and landed next to her in the mud.

Logan attempted to step over the mud puddle but his boot caught the edge of the tank and he went down, too, into the muck. Gunner set the twins on the ground and the boys jumped on top of their father.

"Hey, I want in on the fun." Gunner dived into the mud, spraying everyone in the face.

"Mud fight!" Logan yelled.

"Get Gramps," Reid whispered.

The kids scooped up handfuls of mud and tossed them at the old man. Reid and his brothers joined in. Gramps went over to the spigot on the side of the barn and turned the hose on the group.

"Come over to the grass and I'll hose everyone off," Gramps said.

They lined up and Emmett sprayed them down. Even

Fang got doused with water, then he raced across the yard and up the porch steps.

After Gramps shut off the hose, Reid pointed at Logan. "This is your fault."

Logan shook his head. "You were the one who messed with me on the bucking machine."

Gunner nudged Logan in the side. "And we always thought Reid was a Goody Two-shoes."

"What about us?" Tommy jumped up and down.

Gramps shook his finger at the twins. "You two are big troublemakers."

"I'm heading back to the cabin to change," Reid said.

"I'm going with you, Dad."

Dad. The word acted like a cattle prod, shocking Reid's heart every time he heard it come out of Jessie's mouth. They cut across the yard and she grabbed Fang off the back porch.

Before they climbed into the pickup, she said, "We're gonna get the seats wet."

"They'll dry." He started the engine, then headed down the driveway.

"That was fun," Jessie said.

Reid chuckled. Nothing like a mud fight to resolve a decade's worth of family problems.

"Is Scarlett coming to dinner tonight?" Jessie asked.

"I'm not sure. Why?"

Jessie's happy face turned pensive. "I texted her twice today and she never texted back."

"Was it something important?" he asked.

"No."

"I have a feeling she's really busy with work." He didn't want to share with Jessie that he was just as worried as she was. If Scarlett skipped another family meal, then he was taking matters into his own hands and paying her a visit.

Chapter Thirteen

Scarlett lifted the screaming teakettle from the burner and poured hot water into a mug, then she dunked the teabag up and down.

She glanced at the clock. Seven thirty. Her aunt and Emmett would be back from having dinner at the ranch in another hour. She was going to have to tell her family the truth—that she'd lost her job—but she was so upset and disappointed in herself she couldn't face them yet.

The doorbell rang, but she ignored it. Aunt Amelia was the socialite of the neighborhood and people stopped by unannounced to chat whenever they felt like it. Tonight, they could find someone else to gossip with.

She sat at the kitchen table and blew on her hot tea. No matter how many excuses she came up with for being fired it didn't change the fact that she had no job. Her gaze shifted to the window overlooking the driveway and she let out a squawk when a face stared back at her through the glass. *Reid?* He disappeared and a moment later he pounded on the back door. Why hadn't Lydia or Sadie warned her that he was on his way? She wasn't prepared for this conversation. She flung the door open.

"Scarlett, we need to talk."

Miffed that he'd frightened her, she said, "You're the last person I want to see right now." Then she shut the door in his face.

It opened right back up. Reid stepped into the kitchen, his gaze traveling over her. She tightened the belt on her bathrobe, aware that she looked like the walking dead and he was as handsome as ever.

"You've been avoiding my calls. You haven't answered my texts. And you're not eating dinner with the family. What's going on?"

She dumped her tea out, then washed the cup over and over, keeping her back to him.

"Is it something I did or said?" He stood behind her, crowding her space, forcing her to breathe in his cologne.

She studied his reflection in the window above the sink, trying to decide if it was his kisses or his blue eyes that had been her downfall. He wouldn't leave until he got the answers he came for, so she shut off the water. "It's something we both did."

"How can I make it right?"

"You can't fix it."

He clasped her shoulders. "You're scaring me, Scarlett. Talk to me."

She shrugged off his touch and walked to the other side of the kitchen, keeping the marble island between them. "I was fired from my job today."

His eyes widened. "What happened?"

She crossed her arms over her chest. "I don't want to talk about it."

"You said it was something *we* did."

She watched his face, waiting for him to figure it out on his own. She knew the moment he had—he dropped his gaze and braced his hands against the counter. "Who found out about us?"

"My boss refused to tell me." Scarlett waved a hand in the air. "My best guess is that a coworker saw us together at the carnival."

"We were there with Jessie's family."

"That doesn't matter. We got caught." She drew in a deep breath. "I knew something like this would happen. That's why I warned you we shouldn't cross the line."

"I'm sorry, Scarlett. I didn't think—"

"No." She shook her head. "I'm not blaming you. It's my fault. I knew better and now I have to pay the consequences."

"Isn't firing you a little extreme?" He paced in front of the island. "I'll talk to your supervisor."

"It won't do any good, Reid."

"Why not?"

"This was my second offense."

He stopped pacing and stared at her.

"You don't know the whole story about Dale." She curled her hands into fists. If Dale were here right now, she'd punch him in the throat. "I never told my supervisor in Madison that I was engaged to him. I'd planned to wait until a few months after he got custody of his daughter and the agency closed Amy's case." Her stomach churned. "The judge who granted Dale permanent custody ran into my boss at a social event and asked if Dale and I had set a wedding date yet."

"So you were fired," he said.

"Because it was my first major screw-up, I was offered a chance to resign and my boss suggested I look outside the state for future employment opportunities."

"I'll speak with Mrs. Smith. I'll tell her I put you in a compromising position."

She shook her head. "It won't do any good. My career in social work is over." She waved a hand in the air. "As soon as they assign a new case manager to Jessie, you'll be notified."

She tore her gaze from Reid's. "And it's not just me that's been impacted by my mistake." She made herself look him in the eye. "I won't be able to recommend you receive permanent custody of Jessie. Because of me you'll have to begin the process all over with a new caseworker."

"I don't care about the time frame. As far as Jessie and I are concerned we're already a family and we're sticking together. No judge banging his gavel is going to change that. I'm more worried about you."

Her eyes burned but she refused to cry in front of him. "Maybe I'm not meant to be a social worker."

"Everyone makes mistakes, but you made yours with your heart, not your head."

"Is that supposed to make me feel better?"

He stepped toward her, but she backed up. She couldn't let him touch her or she'd embarrass herself and have a meltdown.

"I've never met anyone with a bigger heart than you, Scarlett. Jessie bonded with you right away. You care about kids and the work you do on their behalf is so important. You can't stop being who you're meant to be."

She shook her head. "That's just it," she said. "I don't know who I am anymore."

"You told me that you went into social work because you wanted to make the world a better place for kids.

Just because you got fired doesn't mean you can't find other ways to champion children."

His words sounded nice, but she was too beat-up inside to appreciate them.

He shoved his hands into his jean pockets. He looked miserable. "There's got to be something I can do."

"I appreciate the offer, but if you get involved you'll make things worse." She wished there was something he could do or say to make this go away. "I allowed this to happen to me twice, Reid. I deserve to be fired."

He grimaced. "I'm not Dale. I didn't use you to get custody of Jessie. I care about you and I'm right here. I'm not going anywhere."

She stared unseeingly across the room. "I'm done talking about this."

After several seconds of silence he asked, "What should I tell Jessie?"

"The truth. Always be truthful with your kid." Scarlett left the kitchen and climbed the stairs to the second floor. She paused on the landing until she heard the back door close, then she went into her bedroom and cried herself to sleep. The next time she opened her eyes sunlight was streaming through the window. She checked the time on her cell phone. Ten o'clock.

A knock sounded on the door, then she heard her aunt's voice asking permission to enter.

"Come in." Scarlett pushed herself into a sitting position.

Aunt Amelia waltzed in, carrying a breakfast tray. She set it over Scarlett's lap. "You look terrible."

"Thank you, Aunt Amelia."

"After you eat, we're going to talk. I'll be back in ten minutes." She left the room.

Scarlett was starving and she finished her food in five minutes. True to her word, Aunt Amelia returned this time with a notepad and a pen. She sat on the fainting couch at the foot of the bed.

"You and I are going to make a new life plan."

"For who?"

Her aunt scowled above the rim of her glasses. "Who do you think?"

Scarlett should have known better than to tell her aunt she'd been fired. "You didn't say anything about my job to Lydia or Sadie, did you?"

Her aunt nodded. "We're family. One for all and all for one."

Scarlett snorted.

"Don't get sassy with me, young lady. Now, let's figure out what you want to do with your life. Would you like to continue working with children in some capacity?"

"I can't imagine myself not being an advocate for kids."

"All right. You're going to continue being a social worker without the title."

"Or the pay."

Amelia smiled. "That's hardly significant. You didn't make much money to begin with, dear."

True. Scarlett hadn't chosen social work because she hoped to be wealthy. Making a child's life better gave her life meaning and made her happy. If she lost that part of herself, she'd feel emptier than ever.

"Where do you want to live?" Aunt Amelia asked.

She traced her fingernail over the flower pattern on the quilt. "I don't know that I can stay here. I might have to move to San Antonio where there are more organizations that help kids."

The pencil moved across the pad. "What about Reid?"

She didn't care to discuss her love life with her aunt. "The rodeo and festival is five days away. Shouldn't you be busy preparing for that?"

"A&B Attractions sent Sadie their proof of insurance so our paperwork is all in order. Lydia arranged for delivery of the portable toilets. Gunner's supervising the setup of the rides Friday morning. Reid's taking care of the fencing for the rodeo on Thursday and the rough stock arrive Friday night. Now quit trying to change the subject." Amelia scowled. "I think you're in love with Reid and you'd like nothing better than to make a life with him and Jessie here in Stampede."

"It's not that simple, Aunt Amelia." Her aunt should know that considering how long she'd waited for Emmett to admit he wanted to be with her.

"Sometimes things happen for a reason. Life is all about taking chances. The problem is most people are too afraid to walk out on that ledge where the view is breathtaking." Amelia scribbled on her notepad and then tore the piece of paper off and handed it to Scarlett.

She read the message, then looked at her aunt. "Are you going to take this advice for yourself?"

Amelia smiled. "I believe I will." She left the room, closing the door behind her.

Scarlett stared at the paper until the words blurred and she could no longer make them out: "Don't let a mistake with one man keep you from being with the man you were destined for."

"HEY, GRAMPS." REID climbed the steps of the front porch late Wednesday afternoon. The old man and Fang sat on the porch swing—the two ornery males were becoming fast friends.

Reid leaned against the rail. "Where is everyone?"

"Logan and Sadie took the kids on a hay ride to test out the new tractor. They'll be back soon."

"Why didn't Fang go along?"

"The goats went with them, so Jessie asked me to babysit the nuisance." His grandfather narrowed his eyes. "How'd things go at the bank?"

"I got the loan. Thanks to Amelia's generous down payment on the property, I didn't need a cosigner." Reid was now the proud owner of the crumbling Amoco station in Stampede.

"You don't seem excited," Gramps said.

He couldn't muster any enthusiasm because he hadn't been able to share the news with Scarlett. He missed seeing her. Missed talking to her. Missed her encouragement. Scarlett was his sunshine and without her his insides felt chilly. "There's a lot of work to do on the building before I open for business."

"Nothing you can't handle."

"It feels surreal."

"Owning a business?" Gramps asked.

Reid nodded. "I remember telling Dad once that I wanted to apply for a job at a lube and oil center in Mesquite. He laughed and said I wasn't smart enough to fix cars."

"You showed him, didn't you?"

Reid had spent hours reading about engines. He'd wanted to prove his father wrong. He'd tried everything he knew how to do to earn his father's love. But nothing he did or said had ever been good enough for Donny Hardell, because Reid hadn't been his biological son.

"All Sara ever wanted for you three boys was to be happy."

"Did Grandma know how you felt about Amelia?"

A deep sigh rattled his grandfather's chest. "My love for Sara was quiet and gentle." He cleared his throat. "When we knew she couldn't beat her cancer, I felt guilty that I hadn't shown my love better through the years. Buying her the motel was my way of saying I was sorry."

"What was her reaction when you told her about the motel?"

The twinkle in his grandfather's eyes returned. "She called me a fool, then she held my hand and told me she didn't want me to be alone the rest of my life."

"So why haven't you and Amelia tied the knot?"

"After Sara passed, it was all I could do to ride herd over you hooligans and run this ranch." Gramps waved a hand in the air. "Besides, what's a woman like Amelia gonna do with a washed-up cowboy like me?"

"I don't know." Reid grinned. "You seem to amuse her."

His grandfather chuckled.

"Stampede is a small town. People talk. Amelia's neighbors are probably wondering what you two are doing when you sleep over at her house. You should make an honest woman out of her."

"She'd never marry me."

"What makes you say that?"

"Never mind about me," Gramps said. "What are you gonna do about Scarlett?"

Reid dropped his gaze. "I screwed up big-time, Gramps, and I don't know how to make it right."

"You talking about Scarlett getting fired?"

"Who told you?" Reid hadn't said a word to anyone, not even Jessie.

"Amelia told Sadie and she told Logan and Logan told me."

That explained the odd looks his family had been giving him the past couple of days. The sound of the tractor engine reached his ears. There wasn't much time to talk so he cut to the chase. "Scarlett and I crossed the line with each other and she got fired because of it."

"Do you love her?"

"I've never felt this way about another woman."

"Is she the first thing you think about when you wake up in the morning and the last thing when you go to bed at night?"

Reid nodded.

"When you see something beautiful like a blooming flower or a colorful sunrise, does it remind you of her?" Gramps was on a roll. "When you learn something new, is she the first person you think about telling? When you see her, does your stomach get the gurgles?"

Reid stretched his arms out. "I can fix a lot of things with these hands, Gramps, but they can't get Scarlett's job back or restore her career in social work."

"How'd they find out about you two?"

"She doesn't know. She thinks one of her coworkers saw us holding hands at the carnival. Whatever the person said they knew about us was enough to get her fired."

A noise behind Reid caught his attention. Jessie stood by the rose bushes looking as if she'd seen a ghost. Fang barked, then jumped off the swing and raced down the steps. Jessie ignored the dog, her expression stricken as she glanced between Reid and his grandfather.

"What's wrong?" Reid asked.

Her lower lip wobbled and tears dribbled from her eyes. Reid left the porch and knelt in front of her. "Did you get hurt?"

"What happened?" Sadie stepped onto the porch, her attention on Jessie.

"It's my fault," Jessie sobbed and threw herself at Reid.

He wrapped his arms around her and held her close.

Sadie came down the steps and stroked Jessie's ponytail. "What is it, honey?"

Jessie wouldn't let go of Reid. "Scarlett got fired because of me."

"No, she didn't, honey. Sometimes these things just happen," Sadie said.

"I told Mrs. Delgado that Scarlett was my dad's girlfriend." Jessie buried her face in Reid's shirt, the sobs growing louder.

Reid hugged his daughter harder.

"I didn't mean to, Dad. I swear I didn't know she'd tell Scarlett's boss."

"Why's JJ crying?" Tommy asked when he came into the front yard with Tyler.

"Emmett, would you take the boys inside and fix them a snack?"

Tyler followed his brother and grandfather into the house and asked, "Is JJ in trouble?"

The question made Jessie cry louder.

Reid tipped her chin up and waited until she made

eye contact. "Scarlett and I are adults. Adults make mistakes."

"Scarlett's not a mistake, Dad," Jessie whispered. "Is she?"

Reid's eyes stung. "No, baby, Scarlett isn't a mistake."

More tears fell. "I don't want her to be mad at me."

"I promise you that Scarlett isn't mad at you, honey," Sadie said.

"Can't her boss forgive her and let her have her job back?"

"There are rules that can't be broken," Reid said. "I'm afraid Scarlett can't work there anymore."

"Can we get her another job?" Jessie looked so hopeful that Reid's heart cracked wide-open.

Sadie gasped and Reid looked up at her.

"There is something we might be able to do."

Jessie wiped her eyes on her shirtsleeve. "What?"

"I'm on the PTO committee at school. The teachers asked us to raise money for special activities for the kids with behavioral problems." Sadie looked at Reid. "What if we use the petting zoo as a program for at-risk kids?"

Reid glanced at Jessie. "And Scarlett would be in charge of running the program?"

"I can't think of anyone more qualified than Scarlett to work with troubled kids," Sadie said.

"It won't be cheap and Scarlett couldn't do it by herself," Reid said.

"We'd have to invest in bathrooms and probably another building for indoor activities but I happen to know a woman who'd be happy to part with more of her money if it means helping families in the community."

"Do you think Scarlett would go for the idea?" Reid asked.

"I don't know. It's up to you two to convince her to spearhead the program." Sadie went into the house.

Jessie tugged on Reid's shirtsleeve. "Can I tell Scarlett, Dad? Please?"

"Let's go back to the cabin and then we'll figure out a plan."

Jessie scooped Fang off the ground, and they all hopped into the truck. "I'm sorry, Dad."

He reached across the seat and squeezed her hand. "You have nothing to be sorry for." He grinned. "I should be thanking you." He laughed at her wide-eyed gape. "If you hadn't come into my life I never would have found out how much I love being your father."

Jessie's smile gave Reid hope that there was still a chance for him and Jessie and Scarlett to be a family.

Chapter Fourteen

"Do you think Scarlett's going to like the ring?" Jessie asked.

"I hope so. But that's why I needed you to help me pick it out." Reid and his daughter were on their way home from a shopping trip in San Antonio. Wednesday night he and Jessie had gone back to the cabin where Reid had confessed that he was in love with Scarlett and wanted to marry her but only if Jessie approved. He'd made sure that Jessie knew that her happiness was his main concern and that he wouldn't propose until Jessie felt comfortable with the idea of the three of them being a family. Jessie had taken all of ten seconds to decide she wanted Scarlett to be her step-mom.

"Was it okay that I picked the more expensive ring?"

Reid laughed. "I don't think you'll hear Scarlett complain about the size of the diamond."

"I just thought if we got her the bigger one, then she'd know we really want to marry her."

While Sadie was quietly working behind the scenes with the PTO members, Reid and Jessie had been making plans to propose to Scarlett. They'd decided to decorate the cabin and invite her over for dinner tonight. On the way through town they'd bought groceries for a spaghetti dinner and a pretty pink cake that Jessie picked out in the bakery.

"Maybe you should give Scarlett the ring before I tell her I'm sorry I told Mrs. Delgado about you guys. Just in case."

His daughter was more nervous than he was.

"Did you memorize what we wrote down?"

"No, but I have the paper in my pocket," she said.

He and Jessie had written the proposal together. "Don't lose it."

"I won't."

"After she says yes, I'll text Aunt Sadie. She said she'd come get me and I could spend the night at the house so you guys can, you know…"

He turned his head away and grinned.

"Can I tell her about the idea Aunt Sadie came up with before I leave?"

"Sure." He turned down the gravel drive, then muttered, "Uh-oh," when he saw who was sitting on the porch.

"What's she doing here?" Jessie asked.

"I don't know." But Scarlett was a sight for sore eyes.

He parked next to her car, then looked at Jessie. "Do we have a backup plan?" His daughter shook her head. "Okay, then. We're going to have to wing this."

As soon as they got out of the pickup, Scarlett left the porch and walked toward them. She wasn't smiling and Reid's stomach clenched, hoping she wasn't about to break his and his daughter's heart.

SCARLETT HADN'T TOLD her cousins that she was paying Reid and Jessie a visit this afternoon, because she hadn't wanted her family poking their noses in her business or telling her what to say or how to say it. She was nervous enough as it was.

She walked over but before she got her first words out Reid spoke.

"How long have you been waiting here?" he asked.

"About an hour."

"We were in San Antonio shopping," he said.

Scarlett glanced between the pair. "Would you mind if I spoke to Jessie in private?"

Jessie sent her father an anxious look and Reid patted her shoulder. "I'll be in the cabin." He grabbed a handful of shopping bags from the pickup and went inside.

"Let's take a walk," Scarlett said. They wandered down the path behind the property until the cabin was no longer in view. "I want to apologize to you, Jessie."

"You do?"

"I'm afraid I used poor judgment in my job and because of that you and your dad are going to be assigned a new caseworker." Scarlett stopped and looked Jessie in the eye. "Which means it's going to take longer for your father to get permanent custody of you. And for that I'm very sorry."

"I'm sorry, too."

"You have nothing to be—"

"It was me." Jessie walked a few feet away, then turned back to Scarlett. "I told Mrs. Delgado that you were my dad's girlfriend."

"When?"

"It was before my Dad and I took the tour of the school. She called me and I was telling her about everything at the ranch and it just slipped out." Jessie got tears in her eyes. "I didn't think I said anything bad."

Scarlett walked over and hugged Jessie. "You didn't do anything wrong, honey."

"But you got fired."

"That's true. I'm no longer a social worker, but I'm confident I'll find another job somewhere else."

"What do you mean somewhere else?" Jessie's voice rose in panic. "Are you leaving? You can't leave."

"I'm not leaving," Scarlett said. "I'm staying in Stampede." Jessie looked visibly relieved and Scarlett drew courage from the girl's reaction. They turned and retraced their steps to the cabin. "I have a serious question to ask and you might think it's silly, but your answer is very important."

"Okay."

"You and your father have just been reunited," Scarlett said. "And I would never want to take your father's attention away from you. One of the things I admire most about your dad is that he always tries to do what's best for you. You and him are a success story and I don't want anything to ever come between you two."

They stopped by the cabin porch. "Are you asking me if it's okay for you to be my dad's girlfriend?"

Scarlett smiled. "Would it be okay if I was more than your dad's girlfriend?"

Jessie's eyes widened and Scarlett said, "It's not just your dad I want to be with. I want to be with you, too, Jessie." She smiled. "I want what's best for all of us. If we're going to be a family, then we're going to stay together through all the ups and downs. It's important to me that you want me to be in your life as well as your dad's."

"I like you a lot, Scarlett. It's okay if you want to be with my dad."

"One of the reasons I love your father is—"

"You love my dad?"

Scarlett nodded.

"Oh, no!"

"What?"

"Dad!" Jessie raced up the porch steps and into the cabin, slamming the door closed behind her.

That went well.

A minute later Reid stepped outside alone and smiled at her.

"This isn't how I'd planned for things to go," Scarlett said.

He came down the steps and stood before her. "And this isn't how Jessie and I had planned for things to go, either."

The situation was growing more confusing by the second. "What do you mean?"

"Jessie and I have been discussing my feelings for you." Reid stared at her as if she was his whole world.

"When you came out of the motel office and plowed into me the first night we met, I thought it was adrenaline making my heart pound. I didn't realize that I was holding on to my future."

Tears welled in Scarlett's eyes.

"I've dreamed of you and I together every night since. I think I knew we were destined for this moment."

"What moment is that?" The question left her mouth in a breathless whisper.

"The moment where I tell you that I love you and that Jessie and I want you to be part of our lives forever."

A tear escaped her eye and Reid brushed the moisture away with the tip of his finger. "You're making this too easy." She smiled despite her watery eyes. "I came here to tell you that I'm done second-guessing myself or trying to talk myself out of how I feel about you because I'm afraid I might get hurt again." She drew in a deep breath. "I love you, Reid. And I want to make a life with you and Jessie, if you'll have me."

"Are you asking me to marry you, Scarlett?"

She nodded.

He pulled a piece of paper out of his pocket and unfolded it. He cleared his throat, then he said, "Jessie and I wrote this out last night." He drew a deep breath. "Scarlett, we need you. Not because you were helping me and my dad stay together, but because you make us feel safe and we know you love us. If you stay, we promise we'll make you happy forever."

Tears dribbled down her face and Scarlett sniffed.

Reid folded the paper and shoved it back into his pocket. Then he took Scarlett's hands in his. "*I* love you, Scarlett. Because you show me each and every day that there's more good than bad in the world. You convinced me that family is worth fighting for. You believed in me, when I had my doubts that I could be the kind of father Jessie deserved. When I'm with you I feel like I can face any challenge. But most of all you make me a better man. I love you and I want to share the rest of my life with you."

She smiled, ignoring the tears that rolled down her cheeks. "Are you asking me to marry you, Reid?"

He pulled a jewelry box from his front pocket and went down on one knee. She gasped when he opened the lid. "Scarlett, will you make me and Jessie the happiest people in the world and marry us?"

"Yes." Smiling she held out her hand and he slid the ring over her finger.

"It's stunning."

Reid stood, then kissed her.

The front door opened and Jessie poked her head out. "Did she say yes?"

Scarlett peered past Reid's broad shoulder. "Yes!"

"Yay!" Jessie ran down the steps and hugged Scarlett.

"Come inside," Jessie said. "We have decorations and Dad and I are going to make you spaghetti for supper. But we have to hurry because Aunt Sadie called and we're supposed to come up to the house so she can tell you about your new job." Jessie raced back inside.

Scarlett grabbed Reid's shirtsleeve. "What new job?"

"Jessie can explain over supper." He slid his arm around her waist and they entered the cabin.

There was a lot to discuss, details to iron out and wedding plans to make. But the most important question had been answered—she, Reid and Jessie were going to be a forever family.

Epilogue

"Uncle Gunner's over there," Jessie said, pointing out the windshield when Reid pulled into the motel parking lot at the crack of dawn Saturday morning. The Stampede Rodeo and Spring Festival kicked off at noon and Gunner was supposed to be keeping an eye on the carnival workers as they tested the rides, but he'd called in a panic and had asked Reid to take over for him.

Four weeks had passed since he and Jessie had arrived in Stampede and so much had happened in the short time they'd been there. Next Monday renovations began on the Amoco station. He hoped to be open for business by the time school let out for the summer. He'd decided to turn the space above the garage into a studio apartment where Jessie could hang out after school with her friends or do her homework while she waited for him to get off work. He'd figured the apartment would get a lot of use when family or friends came to visit.

Sadie and Scarlett were scheduled to meet with the PTO members and school board next week to discuss designing a program at Paradise Ranch for at-risk kids. And yesterday morning Scarlett's boss had phoned him with the news that she'd taken over Jessie's case and would be recommending he receive permanent custody at a court hearing set for the middle of July.

Reid parked the pickup and he and Jessie hopped out. "I got here as fast as I could. What's the matter?"

"Lydia's parents will be here in an hour. They wanted to surprise Lydia, but she had to meet with a client for a couple of hours this morning in Mesquite. I have to go out to the ranch and get the baby from Sadie and take her back to the apartment, before my in-laws arrive."

"Can I ride with Uncle Gunner to the ranch and hang out with the twins?"

"Sure," Reid said.

"I'll be back by the time the carnival kicks off," Gunner said.

"Buckle up," Reid told Jessie.

"I always do, Dad."

He watched the pair drive off, a little amazed that he still got choked up when he thought about his family. Before Reid had a chance to check in with the workers, Amelia drove her white 1958 Thunderbird convertible into the parking lot. As soon as she cut the engine, his grandfather got out and paced in front of the car. Amelia remained behind the wheel, watching with an amused expression.

Reid walked over to the couple. "What's up?"

Emmett pointed to the car, opened his mouth, then clamped it closed again.

Amelia laughed.

"Darn woman is pushier than a—"

"Persistent, not pushy," she said.

Emmett threw his shoulders back and blurted out, "She asked me to marry her."

Reid grinned.

"Emmett's at a loss for words." Amelia quirked an eyebrow. "Help him find his words, Reid."

"It ain't right for the woman to ask. That's a man's job."

"I'll be dead by the time you get up the nerve to propose to me."

His grandfather tugged at his shirt collar as if the material choked him.

"If you ask me," Amelia said, "Emmett's getting the better end of this deal."

"Wait a darned minute." Reid's grandfather stomped over to the driver's door. "I don't give a hoot about your money."

Amelia smirked. "You like the expensive ice cream I buy."

Gramps opened his mouth but she cut him off. "And my soft Turkish bath towels."

Emmett grumbled.

"And you love rolling around naked on my silk bedsheets from Nieman Marcus."

His grandfather's face glowed red when he looked at Reid. "Those sheets are as soft as a baby's butt."

"You two could keep your finances separate," Reid said.

"Why would we do that?" Amelia protested. "I want to travel and it will take Emmett another lifetime to save enough money for a plane ticket to Tibet."

"Why in tarnation would you want to go to Tibet?"

"Haven't you always wanted to meet the Dalai Lama?"

Emmett stared at Reid. "She's losing her marbles."

"You've lived your entire life in Stampede, Gramps. It wouldn't hurt to see a bit of the world."

"I told you that your grandsons would approve," Amelia said.

"You know, you could find yourself a more agreeable man for a travel partner than my grandfather." Reid grunted when the old man elbowed him in the gut.

"I have no idea why Amelia would want to marry an old cuss like you," Reid added with a groan.

Amelia tapped her fingers against the steering wheel. "Because I love him."

His grandfather made a rude noise.

"You know darn well I have loved you since the tenth grade." She waved a hand. "I have loved your stubborn hide for most of my life and whether or not you marry me, won't change how I feel about you."

"Jeez, Gramps," Reid said. "It would be mean not to put her out of her misery."

His grandfather jutted his chin. "I'm still the mayor."

"I know that," she said.

"I'm not gonna let you steamroll me into making more changes in this town."

Amelia's eyes sparkled. "Of course you won't. You'll make me jump through hoops like you always do."

"I'm keeping my truck," he said.

"I'll buy you a new truck. One that doesn't make so much noise."

"I like my truck."

"Fine," she said. "Keep your truck."

The old man's eyes pleaded with Reid. "Tibet?" he whispered. "I'd rather visit the North Pole."

"We can go there, too," she said.

His grandfather stubbed his toe against the ground. "She's not half-bad when she stops yammering."

"Amelia was Grandma's best friend. She'd be happy that you two are together."

He walked up to the driver's side of the car. "Scoot your sassy fanny over. If we're getting married, I'm driving."

"Thank goodness. Now the neighbors will stop calling me a hussy because you park your truck in my driveway every night." She winked at Reid.

"No one calls my gal a hussy," Gramps grumbled. "Who is it? I'll knock their teeth out."

Amelia ran her fingers through Emmett's hair. "They don't have any teeth to knock out, dear. They all wear dentures."

His grandfather started the engine. "We'll be back later after we get married at the courthouse in Mesquite."

Amelia blew a kiss as they drove away in the vintage car. The vehicle hadn't been gone ten minutes when Reid's phone went off.

"I'm almost to the motel," Logan said. "I just passed Gramps and Amelia on the highway."

"Amelia proposed and he said yes."

Logan chuckled. "It's about time."

"They're on their way to Mesquite to get married at the courthouse."

"I better let Sadie know." Logan ended the call.

The rest of the morning passed in a whirlwind and when the carnival kicked off at noon there was already a crowd in attendance. The smell of fried food, popcorn and funnel cakes hung in the air and music blared from the loudspeakers next to the rides.

"When's the rodeo?" Jessie asked after she arrived with the clan.

"It begins in an hour," he said.

Scarlett snuggled against his side. "I'll still love you even if you fall off your horse."

"A rodeo cowboy doesn't fall off, he gets bucked off."

She stood on tiptoe and kissed his cheek. "Don't get hurt."

"I'll try not to." He took money out of his wallet and gave it to Jessie. "You girls get something to eat and find a seat in the stands."

Scarlett gave him another kiss, then whispered in his ear. "If you fall off your ride, later tonight I'll give you another chance to make it to eight on me."

Reid's face grew warm and he chuckled. "I just might fall off on purpose now."

"What's the matter?" Logan asked after Scarlett and Jessie walked off.

Reid grinned at his brother and Logan chuckled.

"You're up first in the bareback competition," Logan said. "Gunner's at the chute. Let's go."

They cut across the parking lot and made their way to the livestock chutes where Gunner flagged them down. "You ready, Reid?" he asked.

"As ready as I'll ever be," he said.

Logan handed him a pair of spurs. "These will bring you good luck. I wore these when I won my buckle."

Reid's throat grew tight. "Thanks."

After he adjusted the spurs, Gunner checked the rigging and handed Reid a pair of gloves. "Our hands are about the same size. Try these on."

The gloves were a perfect fit. Reid nodded to his brothers. "Thanks for looking out for me."

Gunner and Logan exchanged glances, then Gunner spoke. "Now that we got all of our family baggage unpacked, can I stop babying you?"

"Babying?" Reid asked.

"Yeah," Gunner said. "I can say stuff like I'm gonna kick your arse in this competition."

Reid laughed. "Stand back and be amazed, brothers, because I'm going to show you how military cowboys get it done."

The rodeo announcer called Reid's name, and suddenly his brothers were all business, helping him climb onto a bronc named Runaway. They doled out advice and warnings and Reid let them fuss over him. He'd finally come back to Stampede after all these years and all he could think about was why he'd waited so long.

His thoughts flashed back to the day social services had called him about Jessie. The terror he'd felt at being responsible for another human being and then the fierce feeling of protectiveness that swept over him when he met his daughter for the first time. From now on Stampede would be remembered as the place that helped him and Jessie find their way and had brought Scarlett into his life.

The gate opened and Runaway burst into the arena. Reid lasted four seconds before he sailed through the air. He hit the dirt, the air escaping his lungs in a loud grunt. When he climbed to his feet, he snatched his hat off the ground and waved at the stands.

His gaze connected with Scarlett's and Jessie's and in that instant Reid believed he'd claimed the bigger victory today—his own happy-ever-after.

* * * * *

*If you loved this book, look for the
previous titles in Marin Thomas's*
COWBOYS OF STAMPEDE, TEXAS *series:*

*THE COWBOY'S ACCIDENTAL BABY
TWINS FOR THE TEXAS RANCHER*

Available now from Harlequin Western Romance!

We hope you enjoyed this story from
Harlequin® Western Romance.

Harlequin® Western Romance is coming to an end, but community, cowboys and true love are here to stay. Starting July 2018, discover more heartfelt tales of family and friendship from **Harlequin® Special Edition**.

Romance is for life, and these stories show that every chapter in a relationship has its challenges and delights and that love can be renewed with each turn of the page!

Look for six *new* romances every month from **Harlequin® Special Edition!**
Available wherever books are sold.

Get 4 FREE REWARDS!

We'll send you 2 FREE Books plus 2 FREE Mystery Gifts.

Harlequin® Special Edition books feature heroines finding the balance between their work life and personal life on the way to finding true love.

FREE
Value Over
$20

YES! Please send me 2 FREE Harlequin® Special Edition novels and my 2 FREE gifts (gifts are worth about $10 retail). After receiving them, if I don't wish to receive any more books, I can return the shipping statement marked "cancel." If I don't cancel, I will receive 6 brand-new novels every month and be billed just $4.99 per book in the U.S. or $5.74 per book in Canada. That's a savings of at least 12% off the cover price! It's quite a bargain! Shipping and handling is just 50¢ per book in the U.S. and 75¢ per book in Canada*. I understand that accepting the 2 free books and gifts places me under no obligation to buy anything. I can always return a shipment and cancel at any time. The free books and gifts are mine to keep no matter what I decide.

235/335 HDN GMY2

Name (please print)

Address   Apt. #

City   State/Province   Zip/Postal Code

Mail to the Reader Service:
IN U.S.A.: P.O. Box 1341, Buffalo, NY 14240-8531
IN CANADA: P.O. Box 603, Fort Erie, Ontario L2A 5X3

Want to try two free books from another series? Call 1-800-873-8635 or visit www.ReaderService.com.

---

*Terms and prices subject to change without notice. Prices do not include applicable taxes. Sales tax applicable in N.Y. Canadian residents will be charged applicable taxes. Offer not valid in Quebec. This offer is limited to one order per household. Books received may not be as shown. Not valid for current subscribers to Harlequin® Special Edition books. All orders subject to approval. Credit or debit balances in a customer's account(s) may be offset by any other outstanding balance owed by or to the customer. Please allow 4 to 6 weeks for delivery. Offer available while quantities last.

Your Privacy—The Reader Service is committed to protecting your privacy. Our Privacy Policy is available online at www.ReaderService.com or upon request from the Reader Service. We make a portion of our mailing list available to reputable third parties that offer products we believe may interest you. If you prefer that we not exchange your name with third parties, or if you wish to clarify or modify your communication preferences, please visit us at www.ReaderService.com/consumerchoice or write to us at Reader Service Preference Service, P.O. Box 9062, Buffalo, NY 14240-9062. Include your complete name and address.

HSE18

Is that what you want? The question was still there, in his
eyes. All she had to do was decide.

She took a deep breath and shook her head.

Zander leaned closer, his eyes hard on hers. Then he
reached to cup her face with his free hand and drew the
pad of his thumb slowly, deliberately along the swell of
her bottom lip. "Tell me what you want, Allegra."

You. She swallowed. *I want you.*

"This," she said, reaching up on tiptoe to close the
space between them and touch her lips to his.

What are you doing? Stop.

But it was too late to change her mind. Too late to
pretend she didn't want this. Because the moment her
mouth grazed Zander's, he took ownership of the kiss.

His hands slid into her hair, holding her in place, while
his tongue slid brazenly along the seam of her lips until
they parted, opening for him.

Then there was nothing but heat and want and the
shocking reality that this was what she'd wanted all
along. Zander.

Had she always felt this way? It seemed impossible. Yet beneath the newness of his mouth on hers and the crush of her breasts against the solid wall of his chest, there was something else. A feeling she couldn't quite put her finger on. A sense of belonging. Of destiny.

Home.

Allegra squeezed her eyes closed. She didn't want to imagine herself fitting into this life again. There was too much at stake. Too much to lose. But no matter how hard she railed against it, there it was, shimmering before like her a mirage.

She whimpered into Zander's mouth, and he groaned in return, gently guiding her backward until her spine was pressed against the cool marble wall. Before she could register what was happening, he gathered her wrists and pinned them above her head with a single, capable hand. And the last remaining traces of resistance melted away. She couldn't fight it anymore. Not from this position of delicious surrender. Her arms went lax, and somewhere in the back of her mind, a wall came tumbling down.

The breath rushed from her body, and a memory came into focus with perfect, crystalline clarity.

Let's make a deal. If neither of us is married by the time we turn thirty, we'll marry each other. Agreed?

Agreed?

Don't miss
HOW TO ROMANCE A RUNAWAY BRIDE
by Teri Wilson, available July 2018 wherever
Harlequin® Special Edition books and ebooks are sold.

www.Harlequin.com

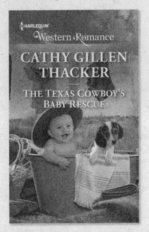

Looking for inspiration in tales
of hope, faith and heartfelt romance?

Check out **Love Inspired**® and
Love Inspired® **Suspense** books!

New books available every month!

CONNECT WITH US AT:

Harlequin.com/Community

ReaderService.com

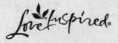

LIGENRE2018

LOVE
Harlequin
romance?

Join our Harlequin community to share your thoughts and connect with other romance readers!

Be the first to find out about promotions, news, and exclusive content!

Sign up for the Harlequin e-newsletter and download a free book from any series at

www.TryHarlequin.com

CONNECT WITH US AT:

Harlequin.com/Community

 Facebook.com/HarlequinBooks

Twitter.com/HarlequinBooks

Instagram.com/HarlequinBooks

Pinterest.com/HarlequinBooks

ReaderService.com

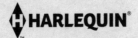 **HARLEQUIN®**

**ROMANCE WHEN
YOU NEED IT**

HSOCIAL2017

Reward the book lover in you!

Earn points from all your Harlequin book purchases from wherever you shop.

Turn your points into *FREE BOOKS* of your choice
OR
EXCLUSIVE GIFTS from your favorite authors or series.

Join for FREE today at
www.HarlequinMyRewards.com.

Harlequin My Rewards is a free program (no fees) without any commitments or obligations.

MYR17